ZIP CODE

LOUIS ROMANO

Copyright © 2017 by Louis Romano
Cover Art Design by Michael Claude

All rights reserved.

Published by Vecchia
All characters and events in this book are fictitious.
All resemblances to persons living or dead are
purely coincidental.

No part of this document may be reproduced or
transmitted in any form or by any means, electronic,
mechanical, photocopying, recording, or otherwise, without
prior written permission of Vecchia Publishing. For
information regarding permission, write to Vecchia Publishing.
Attention: Vecchia Publishing, 41 Grand Avenue, Suite 101,
River Edge, New Jersey, 07661

For classroom BULK ORDERS:
Contact Vecchia Publishing

ISBN-10: 1-944906-08-8

ISBN-13: 978-1-944906-08-5

Printed in the U.S.A.

First Edition, 2017

Also by Louis Romano

Detective Vic Gonnella
(True Crime Series)

INTERCESSION
YOU THINK I'M DEAD
JUSTIFIED

Gino Ranno
(Mob Series)

FISH FARM
BESA
GAME OF PAWNS

Poetry

ANXIETY'S NEST
ANXIETY'S CURE

I have many groups and people to thank for their help and guidance while I was working on this book, but extra special thanks goes to:

Nylah Lisowski, Suzanna Rodriguez, Sydney Matheny, Kelly Herness, Isaac Skoyen, Ciera Dubiel, Maggie Lindberg, and Andrea Sosalla, and their instructor Ms Jessica Neitzel, all from the school district of Whitehall, WI who had invaluable input, especially with the first chapter

And special thanks also to students at Primoris Academy for their insight into how teens tick. They are George Eilender, Julien Jerkovich, Clara Kim, Jaime Kim, Joshua Kindler, Drew Langfelder, Andrew Markov, and Tyler Romeo. Special thanks to their teacher, Cara Ruggiero

And to Bridget Fuchsel, a young lady who was my first test reader and editor of this book who did a more than fantastic job. Thank you

For L.J.

ZIP CODE

Chapter 1

07451

The halls of affluent
RIDGEWOOD, NEW JERSEY HIGH SCHOOL

"I'm ditching. C'mon, let's go!" Ryan said to his friend, Jack.

"No, man, I heard this pep rally was actually going to be good."

"Since when? They are always a bunch of...."

Jack interrupted, "Dude, Crazy Spechler is going to be speaking!"

"Spechler? Well, why didn't you say so? He's the only one who makes this place tolerable. I'm in." Ryan threw his backpack over his shoulder and started walking down the hall with his herd of over-achieving classmates, smiling broadly at one of the girls from his second hour class he planned to ask to the homecoming dance next week.

The halls were filled with students ready to graduate, juniors and seniors at one of the wealthiest schools in the nation. On the fast track since childhood, the pretty girls, wearing all the latest fashions, and the brainiacs and jocks knew there was something different brewing when their parents were also asked to attend this event in the theatre, requested by none other than "Dr." Spechler.

Dr. Spechler is the sociology and history teacher, and a favorite among Ridgewood students and parents. For good reason. He challenges every student to be the best they can be, both as individuals and students, and he has a quirky yet engrossing way about him.

Spechler stood at the podium this day looking more like a crazed professor, not a sociology teacher. Donning a white lab coat with pocket protector, black, horn-rimmed glasses, he stood tapping on the microphone and looking around for a reaction from some of his audience to see if they were able to hear him. A man unknown to the student body and their parents, Principal Enrico Taveleres stood at the ready to be introduced and to help out the insanely intelligent but not commonsensical Dr. in case he started having technical difficulties. The Ridgewood principal was also on hand, black suit and tie, looking like he owned the Boardwalk.

"What the heck is Spechler doing looking like that?" Livia leaned in and whispered to her friend, Jayden.

Jayden laughed, "Who knows? I have a feeling though this is going to even top the time he tried to convince us all to "job shadow" our parents for a week and see what they actually do besides go to work."

"I know, right?"

There were some straggler students coming into the state-of-the-art theatre where some 72 pupils and their parents had gathered, the murmurs still continuing as to what was about to take place.

ZIP CODE

"This better be good," said one of the mothers to another, "I had to miss my spin class for this."

After a few minutes, several requests for, "Shhhh!" were heeded and the principal of Ridgewood High got the 2:20 p.m. assembly underway on a mild, fall day.

"Attention, attention everyone. I want to thank everyone for attending..."

"Good God, just get on with it," was whispered under the breath by several parents. Many students turned and looked at those parents and then nodded in agreement.

"... Dr., I mean Mr. Spechler has an idea." Some of the students laughed, some groaned. "Not just any idea, but also more of a vision. An idealistic vision at that, for you forward thinking students." He paused for effect, took a deep breath, then continued. "Mr. Spechler wants to discover what would happen if two of you, from this great group of students, took your last semester of your senior year and transferred to an urban school where there are zero white students and dare I say, less privilege?"

He knew he had to appeal to the kids first and they would then know how to convince their own parents into allowing them to participate. He'd seen them manipulate their too busy parents many a time before regarding new cars, clothes, and extended trips the kids wanted.

"What life lessons will be learned? How will your lives, and the lives around you be affected?

These two students will live near the selected school, forgoing their suburban community with all the trappings of wealth and privilege. The selected students will have to share this idealism and be very brave as well as very smart."

He paused as the students stood up and started to do The Dab. Senioritis had definitely kicked in.

"Hold on, hold on...there's more. At the same time, two students from the selected school will come here."

This time there was complete silence as both parents and students felt the impact of possibilities. At this moment is when Spechler took the mic.

"Parents. Students." He spoke quietly and slowly. "This is exactly what this experiment is about. Your silence just now is very telling and that's what I want to bring to the forefront. You instantly pondered in your mind what could be the negative consequences of allowing lower income, less privileged, minority people into your... and he grinned as only Spechler could and said, shall I say it, "cracker' neighborhood. The entire theatre erupted in two types of laughter... one for the quirky way in which Spechler always got his points across, and two, nervous laughter because they were embarrassed that he was right.

Only nineteen miles separate Ridgewood High from DeWitt Clinton, but in reality they are as far away from each other as the planet Brooklyn is to Borneo.

ZIP CODE

10468

DeWitt Clinton High School, Bronx, New York

Clothing icon Ralph Loren, Nobel Prize winner in Physics, Robert Hofstader, famed screenwriter Paddy Chayefsky, actor Burt Lancaster, hall of fame basketball star Nate Archibald, and billionaire, real estate developer Paul Milstein are among a long list of over achievers who graduated from DeWitt Clinton, so how could any parent complain? Easily. The problem? That was DeWitt from years long gone by. To say Clinton has seen better days in a gross understatement and now virtually no white students attend this school. The graduation rate is barely 64%, but as a beacon of hope, a new principal, the man standing with Spechler, has implemented the Macy program. That is, there is a special school-within-a-school at Clinton which is attempting to crawl out of an enormous academic hole giving hope for the future of the school and its students. Kids in the Macy program have a ninety-four percent graduation rate. In the past two years, four Gates Scholarship awards, giving full rides through their PhD level, have been granted to four DeWitt Clinton students as well as Posse Scholarships granted to several other well-deserving pupils. Clinton is slowly attempting to return to a viable place for learning. Not an easy task for a faint of heart educator.

"Since we have established safety as a concern, let me console you by saying that the parent of one of the Clinton students, a single mom, is a New York City Police Sergeant. I assure you, your child living with one of New York's finest should allay any of your concerns."

None of the kids from Ridgewood who were listening even thought about their security. They believed very strongly in the social experiment. The idea of learning the reality of want vs need, of not having every comfort handed to them, was compelling to these privileged kids. However, it was the naturally protective parents who needed to sign the permission documents.

None was expecting to hear what Spechler said next. "Let me assure you, the parents of the DeWitt students have fears also." Haughty gasps were heard by a few, but then stone-cold silence once again filled the room as Spechler continued. "Their children are tough and street smart, unlike some of ours here, but they are minorities coming to suburban America, which we all think of as safe--but is actually an environment they fear.

The winter session of the Spechler Experiment was to begin on Monday, January 4, 2016. If, after promises of 6 paid for college credits amounting to saving several thousands of dollars, and an addition to their child's resumé which could never be beat by anyone else's kids in the country, and two sets of parents agreed, the reality of the social experiment would begin.

"So, who's in it for "the experiment"? Spechler said while laughing and tugging on his white lab coat for effect.

Months before, the Ridgewood school district members, after a thirty-minute private meeting, had decided they would vote unanimously for the program but would take no responsibility for the Spechler Program participants. Any risk was purely on the shoulders of the students and their families. Ridgewood High School, in legal jargon, would be held harmless. The district's lawyers were asked to prepare the appropriate paperwork. It was amazing it actually remained a secret and was not exposed by some of the influential men who also sat on the school board.

ZIP CODE

Several parents, not to be outdone by the other, quickly ushered their children home to make tentative plans to be the ones selected. The successful career tracks put in place since their precious children were toddlers was only part of their ambition to be a part of this program; the money saved on college tuition really meant nothing, especially to the mothers. What was at stake was their need to show the world how inclusive they could be. Not prejudiced. Not judgmental. Not haters and race baiters. But while most parents from Ridgewood were jockeying for position, some parents were not at all concerned as they had already been privately asked to be a part of the program. They were used to the privilege of the rigged game and always enjoyed it. Unfortunately, this time it put them in a spot. As school and community leaders, the school's principal, Dr. Connelly, fully expected the Taylor and Darby families to participate when asked. Privilege does sometimes come at a cost when image is everything.

LOUIS ROMANO

Chapter 2

The parents of A.J. and Logan had decided to meet for dinner to discuss their children going to DeWitt Clinton High School in the Bronx for their final semester. Their children were the brightest of the bright and already had the best chance of being in the social experiment without even asking -- because of their financial influence they had over the school by donating hoards of money each and every year, but things weren't going according to the school's smooth plan.

The two sets of parents met at Café Panache restaurant in affluent Ramsey, New Jersey. A bring your own bottle, French restaurant, Café Panache is the place to be seen, and a chance for these well to do people to drink and display the fine wines from their personal wine cellars. They were seated at their usual table.

"Let's face the fact we can't keep sheltering our kids from the rest of the world. Next year they will be on their own at college. So why not let them have this experience?" Arthur Taylor, A.J.'s dad said.

"Art, I understand that, but the South Bronx? I'm not happy about our kids being in harm's way every day," Kathy Darby, Logan's mom stated.

"I, for one, think this whole program is stupidity. What will it prove? These people are not going to excel like our kids. Jesus Christ, your daughter is gorgeous. Aren't you afraid that she will be a mark for these savages on the streets of the Bronx?" Kyle Darby said. He took a long pull from the expensive, French Boudreaux he brought from home.

"I agree with you Kyle, but my daughter is very headstrong and this is what she really wants to do. I don't agree with it, but I don't know how to stop her," Lilly Taylor said.

"Just say no, for Christ's sake. That's the problem with our kids. They don't know the meaning of the word no. Don't you think it's time we get tough?" Kyle Darby said. He drained his glass and began to pour more of the dark, red wine into his long stem crystal glass.

"And how will they feel about passing up what can be a meaningful experience in their lives? Besides, they get good resumé cred and six credits toward their Bachelor's degrees." Arthur Taylor noted.

"Sorry, but I have to say this, Arty. That's a crock of shit. Pardon my blunt talk here. Neither of us needs the six credits financially. A.J and Logan's resumés are just fine as they are. There will be plenty of other opportunities for them to impress future employers," Kyle Darby said.

Again, he took a long gulp of from his glass. He wasn't savoring the fine wine. He was using the alcohol to help speak his mind. Arthur Taylor reached for his bottle, a costly Super Tuscan, the second bottle before the four parents even looked at the menu, and poured four, fresh glasses, one for each parent.

"My daughter is very naïve. She has no idea what she is getting into. A.J. loves that Mr. Spechler, and has drunk the liberal Kool-Aid he has been spewing for years at Ridgewood. I, for one, really do not care about the kids in the ghetto. They are there for a reason and they are underachievers. I disagree with my husband. We've been arguing about this program for weeks," Mrs. Taylor said.

ZIP CODE

"Is this what we want to teach our children? That they are better than other people because their parents have done well or simply because they are not Hispanic or black or some other minority?" Arthur Taylor said. He flashed a look at his wife to show his disdain for her comments.

"I, for one, do not offer an apology for our family's success. Staying in that god-forsaken neighborhood is not at all where I see my son spending his last semester of high school. Look, we have worked hard to get what we have. We are not anything like the third and fourth generation of these people taking welfare," Lilly Taylor said. Her wide eyes showed her fury.

Both bottles of wine were nearly drained. The waiter came to the table to see if the parents were ready to order their dinner. Lilly Taylor mouthed, *not yet*, to their server.

"So we are better than these people who have the right as American citizens to educate their children and improve upon their personal situations? Think outside the box for a second, will ya? Maybe, just maybe, our kids can help improve our society by bridging the gap between the poor and the affluent," Arthur Taylor said.

"You sound like Karl Marx, or maybe Barack Obama, Arty. These people have no shot at rising to our level. None, whatsoever." Kyle Darby leaned back in his chair and folded his arms. His body language said he was not budging on his opinions.

"I agree with you again, Kyle. This is an exercise in futility. We should just put our foot down, say no, and step in front of this program." Lilly Taylor nearly turned her back from her husband who sat at the table next to her.

"What makes us any better than these people? Because we are all white? Because we were able to get a good education without being pigeon holed as a minority, and put into a failure chain? I, for one, am proud my daughter and your son want to do something about prejudice which continues to disenfranchise the less fortunate in our society." Arthur Taylor's voice rose to a point that a couple at the next table took notice.

"I never would have guessed you were such a liberal, bleeding heart, Arty," Kyle Darby stated.

"Oh, he's always wanting to help the poor, unfortunate underdog, Kyle. And now he is willing to throw his own daughter into that snake pit and risk her life to help the hopeless." Lilly Taylor's tone was a sarcastic and direct attack on her husband.

"I'm going to the school board to put an end to this bullshit once and for all. I've heard all I need to hear. Your wife is right on point, Arthur," Kathy Darby said. She reached her hand across the table to touch Lilly's trembling hand.

"I'm signing that permission letter. What makes the three of you any better than anyone else? Your money? Your big ass house? All your stuff? Let me tell you what I think about this whole conversation. I see no difference between the four of us sitting here, drinking eight hundred dollars worth of these smashed grapes, than four people standing in front of a bodega in the Bronx, drinking whatever the hell they drink out of bottles or cans covered by paper bags. Excuse me, but I've lost my appetite." Arthur Taylor stood up, tossed a fifty-dollar bill on the table to tip the waiter, and left Café Panache without his wife.

CHAPTER 3

Arthur Taylor stopped at a table to greet some friends on his way out of Café Panache. He didn't want to look as if he was storming out of the place, to feed into the rumor mill, but he had no intention of taking the ten-minute drive back home with his wife.

Arthur used his cell phone and was in an Uber car within minutes.

The three other parents lingered at the table for a while, finishing a third bottle of wine, then a fourth. They ordered some appetizers to absorb the alcohol before leaving. Lilly Taylor practiced what she preached to her kids about drinking and driving. Lilly also called for an Uber, leaving her car in Ramsey, to be retrieved the next day.

Arthur was in his study reading a T. J O' Connor mystery, while listening to his favorite Alicia Keys CD when his wife arrived home.

"I had to take a Uber," Lilly said.

"Yeah, me too."

"Sweetie, I'm so sorry I behaved so poorly. We are just at opposite sides of the spectrum on this, and I am afraid for A.J." Lilly nestled next to her husband who was sitting on his oversized, brown, leather chair.

"Don't you think I'm worried for her, Lil? In August, A.J. will be at Brown University. I can't even imagine she is old enough to be going to college. Don't you think there are dangers there, too? Men, drinking, God knows what all? She needs to do what compels her. This thing in the Bronx will define her as a person, Lil. A.J. will get to see a whole different world. The little birdie needs to fly from the nest," Arthur said.

"But the damn Bronx, Arthur? That place is a hellhole. How can these people even live there? I won't be able to sleep while A.J. there," Lilly's voice began to quiver.

"Honey, please stop, you are over dramatizing this thing. We need to let her follow her ambitions. She wants to study Psychology and Sociology. Maybe she wants to be a Psychologist, a teacher, someday be a mom, who knows? This semester will help her enormously. A.J. will emerge as a totally well rounded individual. We owe her this opportunity, Lil," Arthur said.

"In the Bronx? Can't they find another place for this thing?"

"Like where? Camden? Paterson? Or some other underprivileged city? It was fine with you when A.J. went to Barcelona for two weeks last year. Why did she go there?"

"For her A.P. Spanish class," Lillian blurted.

"Yes, and for much more than just language. A.J. went there to learn how to live. To see another culture, to see art, history, try different foods, meet different people. I fail to see this as very different."

"I will never forgive myself if something happens to our precious daughter," and Lillian began to cry.

ZIP CODE

Arthur put his arm around his wife to comfort her.

"Lil, do you have any faith in your daughter? A.J. is no pushover. This is an educational experience. I don't see her smoking crack on a street corner or joining a gang. She really wants this, and we can't stand in her way for our own ideas and prejudices. Enough of this whimpering, Lil," Arthur was tender, yet firm.

"Fine. I will pray on this for a while. I'm starting to feel ashamed of myself if I'm being totally honest. I'm sorry, honey."

"Sorry? You have no need to apologize for your feelings, Lil. I'm very proud of you, and always will be. I should be sorry for walking out on you at the restaurant."

"That was the first time you've ever done something like that to me. I guess we were ganging up on you."

"Kyle and Kathy Darby are not my favorite human beings on the planet. I never liked them from when A.J. played little league baseball. They were all against girls playing in the league if you recall. I saw a real argument coming tonight. I didn't know what else to do, so I left."

"I'll tell you here and now, I will do my best for these two kids that are coming to stay with us. Maybe I can learn something as well," Lilly wiped her tears and kissed her husband on his cheek, gently placing her head into his chest.

"Logan, you are not going to live in the Bronx and go to that disgusting failure of a school next semester. I'm not signing that paper," Kathy Darby screamed.

The Darby's were having breakfast in their immense, tumbled marble and granite-encased kitchen. The school and workday were about to get started. Mrs. Darby was dressed for her morning Pilate's class.

"Mom, A.J.'s parents signed the permission for her to participate in this study. How is that going to look for me? Logan Darby's mommy and daddy said he has to stay in Ridgewood where it's safe and then he can go off to Princeton, where it's safe. Jesus Christ, mom, I want to do this. It's important to me. It may work out that the program is an important mark on our social understanding for years to come. I want to be a part of that."

"A.J.'s dad is a limousine liberal. That's the worst kind of liberal there is," Kathy blurted.

"Wrong, a liberal Jew is the worst," Kyle Darby interrupted.

"Just listen to you two! It's a wonder I don't join the KKK or become a skinhead. The prejudice around here is over the top," Logan said.

"I'm going over to see the principal today, and if I don't get any satisfaction from Dr. Connelly, then I'm going to the School Board. This thing is just dangerous," Kathy stated, emphasizing her opinion by slapping her hands together.

"So I will be totally embarrassed and mortified for the rest of my freakin' life. No way. I'm going to do Mr. Spechler's program and that's the end of it. Sign the freakin' paper. I'm late for school," Logan said. He pointed to the permission letter that was on the kitchen table.

"Screw it, Kathy. What's the worst thing that happens? He knocks up some spic girl and we have to pay for the kid for the rest of our lives. Sign the damn paper," Kyle said. He never took his face away from the Wall Street Journal article on oil fracking he was reading.

"Kyle, really? Do we need that kind of talk at the breakfast table? Pregnant? Really. Kyle knows what he needs to do to protect himself."

"Are you both crazy? Your world has passed. I don't think like you do. I don't hate. I don't think I'm better than anyone who has less than I do," Logan said.

"But you are! You are better than most people, and get that into that knuckle head of yours," Kyle shouted, still never looking up from his newspaper.

"Mom, Dad... either you let me do this project or I'll take next year off and get a job. Columbia can wait," Logan threatened.

"Over my dead body. You've worked since the third grade to get into an Ivy and you are going to give it away now after early acceptance and everything? Have you lost your mind, Logan?" Kathy said.

"Wait Kath, let me check the insurance policy before you kill yourself, I want to make sure we're covered," Kyle laughed.

"Kyle, this is serious, I need you to support me on this," Kathy yelled.

"Mom, I'm serious. You may be able to force me not to join Mr. Spechler's program but you can't force me to go to Columbia in August."

"Are you kidding me right now? This is a bad dream!" Kathy shouted.

"Sign the damn paper," Kyle moaned.

"I'll sign it, but understand a few things. If anything happens to you or your scholarship to Columbia, I'm leaving both of you. I worked my ass off to get you to that place since you were eight years old, and second, don't expect me to have any of these...these people...into my home. Not happening," Kathy said furiously.

She scribbled her name on the document and stormed out of the house into her red, BMW convertible and headed to her workout.

ZIP CODE

CHAPTER 4

07451

Ridgewood, New Jersey

The two, Bronx honor students, Rosa Colon and Semaj Henry, arrived at the Ridgewood train station at eleven o'clock in the morning, the day before classes were to start at their new high school.

Unlike A.J. and Logan, who were personally driven to the Bronx by Logan's father and mother, Rosa and Semaj had to take a variety of subways from the Bronx. They then took a train from Grand Central Station in Manhattan, to Ridgewood.

Lilly Taylor, A.J.'s mom, met the Bronxites on the platform of the Ridgewood station with gifts for both students.

Mrs. Taylor's new, shiny, black Range Rover was parked outside the station in a no-parking zone, emergency flashes blinking away. She and her husband were well known among the twenty-six members of the Ridgewood Police Department, so there was no worry about getting a ticket for illegal parking. The Taylors were extremely generous to the local PBA and a variety of other charities.

"Welcome to Ridgewood, kids. It's nice to finally meet you both. Some flowers for you Rosa, and a cute, Maroons High School teddy bear, the school's mascot. For you Semaj, a hoodie jacket, in maroon with black Ridgewood letters of course. After all, you will now be part of the Maroons for the new semester," Mrs. Taylor said, her wide, gleaming smile showed her sincere caring for her new boarders.

"This is the only time other than my First Holy Communion that I received flowers. Thank you so much," Rosa said. Her large, brown eyes had just a hint of moisture.

Mrs. Taylor, Rosa, and Semaj climbed into the SUV.

"Thank-you, Mrs. Taylor. I'm happy to meet you, too. Thank you for the great shirt," Semaj said.

"You are both very welcome. Well, lets get you back to our home. We have so much to discuss and prepare you for the first day of your last semester of high school. Semaj, I understand you will be going to Hunter College in the fall...that's wonderful! And Rosa, you received a full ride at Fordham University! Mr. Taylor is a Fordham alum. I'm sure he will tell you all about his days there. Matter of fact, he is board member at Fordham now."

"Wow. I can't wait to meet him," Rosa said. Secretly, she was a bit intimidated by that fact that Mr. Taylor was such a big shot.

Rosa looked very much like her mom. A beautiful, round, Latina face, but unlike Sonia, Rosa had a few extra pounds on her five foot two inch frame. Rosa carried a "spare-tire" around her middle that she cleverly cloaked with blousey tops.

"Semaj, I have to ask you. What an interesting name you have? I've never quite heard of it before," Mrs. Taylor asked.

ZIP CODE

"My mom wanted to name me James, after the Apostle. She is very religious, but because I have an older cousin named James, Semaj is James, spelled backward," Semaj said. A hint of pride rose in his voice for having such a unique first name.

Semaj is a tall, incredibly handsome, light skinned African-American. The product of a single mom, Semaj never met his father and was incredibly devoted to his mother and her Christ Alive Christian Church.

"How interesting," Mrs. Taylor said. She was trying to process why a parent would name their child with that sort of name.

The five-minute ride to the Taylor residence, in the affluent hills of Ridgewood, while listening to a CD of Vivaldi's *Four Seasons,* was only a glimpse of a brave new world for Semaj and Rosa. As Mrs. Taylor zipped by the manicured estates, the two Bronx students had all to do to absorb what they were seeing.

"Well, here we are, kids. You're new home for the next twenty weeks. We call it "May as Well," Mrs. Taylor announced.

"How did you get that name?" Semaj asked.

"Well, every time we added an addition, or made some changes to the landscaping we would say, may as well do it. Hence the name," Mrs. Taylor laughed as if spending money were nothing to be concerned about.

Semaj glanced quickly at Rosa with a raised eyebrow that said, "WTF?"

The house is amazing. A massive eight-bedroom Colonial home, including four garage doors, with a wrap around, cobblestone driveway, surrounding gardens with waterfalls, and modern iron and bronze statuary accenting the manicured, sprawling lawns.

"What a beautiful home, Mrs. Taylor," Rosa said. She couldn't even imagine living in a place such as this.

"Let's get you two settled in, then I'll give you the cook's tour." The two teens had no idea what she meant by that, but they *were* hungry.

They stepped in through the main door to the house. Rosa remembered when Dorothy entered the Land of Oz and everything exploded from black and white into Technicolor.

The large foyer was gleaming from the sunlight which bounced off the white, Terrazzo marble floors. A massive, crystal chandelier, illuminating the fine paintings which hung on the ex- quisitely papered walls, accentuated a pinkish hue in the marble. The light tan, leather wallpaper with a hint of pink to pull out the colors in the marble, surrounded two, winding staircases, which led to a second level balcony. Rosa and Semaj just stood there, mouths agape waiting for someone to pinch them.

"Arthur, we're home," Mrs. Taylor announced.

Arthur Taylor entered the foyer from his study, a glass of Scotch in his hand, wearing a Fordham University tee shirt, a pair of slim fit designer jeans and burgundy Italian loafers without socks. At forty-nine, his trim physique and distinguished salt and pepper hair belayed the fact this man was successful and wealthy.

ZIP CODE

"Hey, guys. Welcome home. I trust you had a good trip here," Mr. Taylor said. He shook Semaj's hand with a powerful, manly grip and gently kissed Rosa on her cheek. Rosa felt a bit awkward.

"So Rosa you are going to Fordham next fall. I have a soft spot for any Ram. I took my undergrad degree at the Rose Hill campus. And you will be a biology major, I understand. What is your career track?" Mr. Taylor asked.

"Pre-med, sir. I want to be a pediatrician," Rosa said. There was a hint of nervousness in her voice.

"Fantastic. I will introduce you to the head of internal medicine at Hackensack University Hospital. Doctor Sam Sahoo is a golf buddy of mine. We need bright young women like you to take good care of our future generations. How about you, young man?"

Semaj had to lick his lips and clear his throat to speak.

"Information technology. I like the computer field," Semaj said. He could barely get the words out.

"Fabulous. Hunter is a good school for that field. If you need an apprenticeship, one of my clients is Microsoft. Bill Gates and I are friends. Just make sure your grades are top shelf."

"Yes, sir, I will," Semaj said.

Mrs. Taylor clapped her hands once and motioned to the staircase like she was presenting an Academy Award. "Okay kids, let me show you up to your rooms. Each one of you has your own bathroom in your room so I think you will be very private and comfortable here. Then I'll show you around the place."

"Then we're going over to Varka for an early dinner. I hope you both like good, Greek food," Arthur Taylor said.

"Yes, um, sure," Rosa said.

"Thank-you," Rosa and Semaj answered in unison.

Mrs. Taylor led the students up the large staircase to their respective rooms which were across a wide hallway from each other.

"When you're finished unpacking, find your way down to the kitchen. I have a few snacks ready in case you're hungry, then we can chat about tomorrow," Mrs. Taylor said.

"Thank-you, ma'am," Semaj said.

As soon as Mrs. Taylor left them, Rosa checked the hallway to see if Mrs. Taylor was gone. Semaj, did the exact same thing. From the doorways of their rooms they looked at one another in disbelief.

"Dude, this place is amazing," Rosa said.

"It's out of a book. The Great Gatsby, an' shit," Semaj said.

"How rich is this guy?" Rosa asked.

"No clue. But he seems nice. They both seem nice. Mrs. Taylor is a hottie." Semaj laughed.

ZIP CODE

"Shut up, Semaj. Listen, I have to text and Snapchat my friends. No one would believe this place.

"Good idea, I'm sending my group a text, too," Semaj said.

"I feel sorry for their daughter living in my mom's two-bedroom on Fox. They will be in more shock than I am," Rosa said.

Rosa texted her four, best friends on her iPhone:

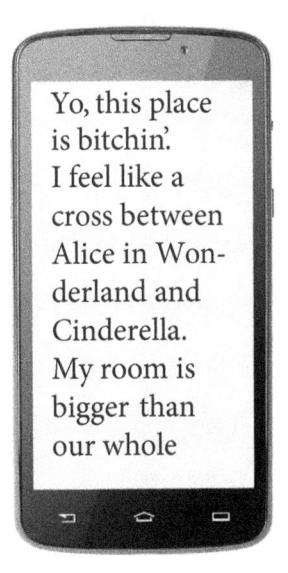

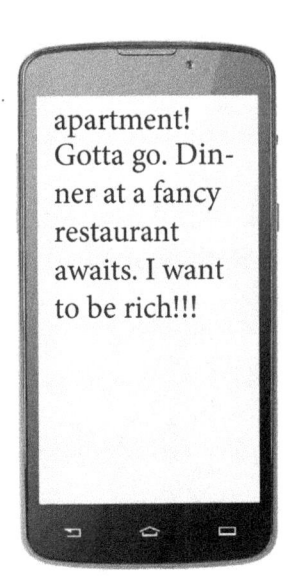

> Yo, this place is bitchin'. I feel like a cross between Alice in Wonderland and Cinderella. My room is bigger than our whole apartment! Gotta go. Dinner at a fancy restaurant awaits. I want to be rich!!!

Semaj's message to his friends was similar. He group texted to 7 of his pals:

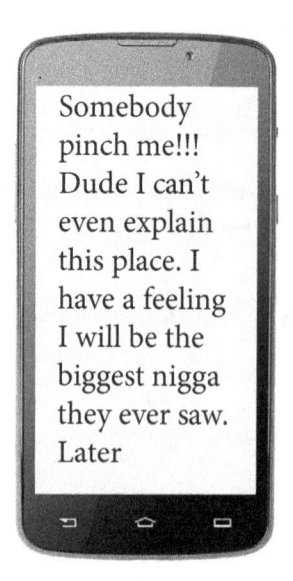

> Somebody pinch me!!! Dude I can't even explain this place. I have a feeling I will be the biggest nigga they ever saw. Later

And Semaj and Rosa hadn't even begun to sample their new life in Ridgewood.

CHAPTER 5

10455

970 Fox Street Bronx, NY

"Well guys, this is what Puerto Ricans eat when we are broke. I'm not broke at the moment, but I want to give you the whole experience. We call it *Arroz blanco con habichuela y huevo frito,* Sounds a lot better in Spanish. White rice with fried eggs."

Sonia Colon made a lunch for her two, new boarders from Ridgewood High School. Sonia is a tough, no-nonsense, NYPD sergeant assigned to the rough 43rd Precinct in the southeast Bronx. At five feet four inches, her black hair pulled back into a tight ponytail, she had to be tough to compete with the male cops, who gave her no breaks since she started on the force six years ago.

Alexandra Jane Taylor and Logan Darby both looked at the meal like it was a dinner at the best five-star restaurant.

"It looks delicious, Sonia. I've never had anything like this," A.J. said. Her big, sky blue eyes were wide with excitement. She moved her long, blonde hair behind her back before digging in.

"What's this drink, Sonia?" Logan asked.

"One of our many traditional drinks. *Cola Champagne.* I thought we would celebrate your arrival. I have some *tres leches* for desert. Homemade...my momma's recipe. We can have a Manhattan Special with that, Sonia said. Her smile made her brown, almond eyes and high cheekbones extenuate her Latina look.

"Manhattan Special? What's that?" A.J. asked.

"It's sort of a coffee-soda. Like a delicious jolt of caffeine."

"Just what I need. I didn't sleep much last night. I guess I was excited about coming here," Logan said. At six feet one inch with a strong, athletic look, Logan is the image of a television soap star. His dark, brown hair and green eyes still had a boyish innocence which made him very popular among the girls at Ridgewood.

"Excited or scared?" Sonia asked.

"Maybe a bit of both to be totally honest. I've never lived anywhere else except Ridgewood," Logan confessed.

"Me either. I stayed at Princeton with my older sister a few times for a weekend, but I guess that doesn't count," A.J. added.

"Not nearly. You will both have to have your wits about you. My advice to you both is to try to look like you belong even though you don't. Never look afraid and never be afraid to run. Remember, a good run is better than a bad stand. A.J. you will get cat calls, whistles, and that horrible kissing sound Latin men make when they see a pretty girl. Ignore them. Don't smile, don't tell them off...just ignore them. Logan, you will be challenged from time to time. Never fall into the trap of being macho. Walk away, unless of course you are put in a position to fight. Then fight hard," Sonia said.

"How are the trains?" Logan asked.

ZIP CODE

"Pretty safe. They have their moments and some creeps, but the trains will be crowded when you need to go to and from school. Mostly with students like yourselves...well almost. Right after lunch, we will take a dry run to Clinton. We will be taking the number six-train to 125th Street in Harlem; going downstairs to the number four train. That takes you to Mosholu Parkway and Jerome Avenue. It's the El, and then it's a two-block walk to the school. I want you to always travel together. I'm insisting on it. No wavering from this rule will be tolerated. If for any reason you need to separate, I want to know about it. Remember, I'm a cop with a lot of friends. If you have a problem use my cell phone. Don't hesitate to call or text me."

"Do we pay for the train tickets each time?" A.J. asked.

"No. I will be giving you a Metro Card which comes out of your allowance. You'll see. Just swipe the card, it's easy," Sonia said as she dished out the rice and egg dish.

"This is delicious," Logan said. He was wolfing down the meal like he was about to go to the electric chair.

"Thank you. It's simple, but good. Don't worry; I'm on the eight to four shift so I'll be home to cook for you guys. I promise to only cook Puerto Rican food for you. Unless we take out. I know a great *Mofongo* house nearby," Sonia said.

"*Mofongo?*" A.J. asked.

"Sounds exotic." Logan added.

"Actually it's Puerto Rican and African. Its mashed fried plantains with a few different spices. It may be an acquired taste for you guys, but you know, 'when in Rome do as the Romans'. Sonia laughed at her analogy.

"Any curfew, Sonia?" Logan asked.

"Did you ever hear that there are no dumb questions? Well, that is a dumb question. Of course there's a curfew. You will have the same restrictions I've given to my daughter. Home after school for homework. I think you will have less of it than your school, but I insist you do it before going out. Supper is at six. After that you need to get your asses back here by nine on school days. We can talk about weekends, but Rosa is usually home at eleven. I don't see me extending that. I want to see how you both do for a while," Sonia said. Her eyes went from A.J. to Logan with no hint of comfort.

"No problem. Just wanted to know," Logan said.

"Okay, you guys can do the dishes. That's my rule. I cook, you clean, and I don't have a dishwasher. I don't care if you make your beds or not. Just don't expect me to do it for you." Sonia meant business.

"We really want to thank you for opening up your home to us. I can't believe I have butterflies in my stomach," A.J. admitted.

"You are very welcome. Have you guys ever been to the Botanical Gardens?"

"Not me. I've been to the Zoo a couple of times with my folks," Logan said.

"Nope. I think the only time I've ever been to the Bronx was with my dad to see the Yankees play," A.J. added.

"If you like, we can shoot over there after we take the ride to the school. Unless you think it's not cool."

"Absolutely! I want to go. Whatever we can learn about the Bronx would be great," A.J. said.

"Sure, why not? Are they open on Sundays?" Logan asked.

"'Till six," Sonia replied.

"I guess that's another dumb question," Logan laughed.

"Not at all. I've lived here my whole life and had to Google it this morning," Sonia laughed even harder.

As planned, Sonia took A.J. and Logan to the subway station on 138th Street and Cypress Avenue in the Bronx. They caught the number six-train to 125th Street in Harlem and transferred to the number four-train back up to the Bronx.

This being a Sunday, the trains were relatively empty and quiet. A.J. and Logan were the only non-Latino or black passengers on the train until they transferred on 125th Street Station where only a hand full of white people were seen.

On the number four-train, Sonia began a more detailed tutorial.

"Now, tomorrow the trains will be pretty busy. It's a workday and a school day, so try to grab a seat as quickly as you can. If you can't find a seat, which is likely, just hold on to one of these poles for balance," Sonia said.

Sonia pointed to a map inside the train to show the wide-eyed students the route they would be taking.

"The trip to Clinton should take about forty minutes baring any track or train problems. There will be a good amount of Clinton, Bronx High School of Science, and Lehman College kids on this train, and everyone is in the same boat. They all want to get to school and start their day, so the atmosphere will be pretty somber. It's early morning, a new semester is beginning, and the holiday break was way too short, so there will not be too many happy faces," Sonia advised. She spoke so quickly it was as if it were all one word.

"Wait. What? What stop will get off again?" A.J. asked.

"We will be there in a few minutes. Mosholu Parkway and Jerome Avenue. The train will empty out at the station," Sonia said. She remained quiet the rest of the way until they reached their destination.

"See? Pretty simple," Sonia said. A.J. and Logan were not so easily convinced.

"I hope this comes back to me in the morning," A.J. said to herself. She was already beginning to wonder if this was a good idea after all. Then her optimism kicked in. A.J. felt in her heart she was doing the right thing for a better, more understanding society.

"Now we go down the long flight of stairs to the street. Tomorrow, just keep up with the crowd. Don't be looking around like you are two hayseeds from Kansas," Sonia laughed.

ZIP CODE

Logan thought, *What the hell does she mean by that? Does she think we can't fit in this oh-so-tough-guy neighborhood?* Out loud he said, "No, we are just hicks from New Jersey." His quip was not meant to be funny.

"There's the school. Let's stand here for a minute so I can give you the local geography. Clinton has several natural boundaries which surround it. As you can see, it's not in the hood. Over there is busy Mosholu Parkway. During the summer, there are lots of people in the park right there having picnics, sunning themselves, studying, hanging out, kicking soccer balls, or playing catch, that sort of thing. Behind Clinton is Bronx Science. Mostly Asian brainiacs. It's one of the best high schools in the city. From what Rosa tells me, Bronx Science kids keep pretty much to themselves. Then behind us is Van Cortland Park. It's a huge public park for sports, horse riding, a golf course, picnics...all kinds of recreational things. On the side of Clinton there is the Jerome Reservoir. Then way up on that hill is Woodlawn Cemetery. It's a massive graveyard. Herman Melville, Damon Runyon, Irving Berlin, and a whole bunch of other people are buried there," Sonia said.

"The Bronx was pretty famous back in the day," A.J. said.

"It was, and then it nearly burned to the ground. It was a great place for me to grow up, and it's really starting to come back, but slowly," Sonia said.

It was a crisp, but sunny day, and the three of them began walking toward DeWitt Clinton.

"That school is huge!" Logan stated.

"Oh, yeah. I guess it runs more than two or three city blocks in every direction. The athletic fields behind the school are massive. Don't forget, at one time it was one of the most populated schools in New York City, if not the largest," Sonia said.

"This is not at all what I expected. You're right Sonia, it's surrounded by a lot of amazing places, and it really looks like a great place," A.J. said. Secretly, she was a bit intimidated by the sheer size of the campus.

"It's amazing. I'm going to need a map of the place to find my classes." Logan said. He also was a bit nervous about tomorrow, but kept his male bravado in place.

"I called a friend of mine who is stationed in the precinct here and she promised to meet us and get you guys a look inside. There she is, in the patrol car in front," Sonia said.

"Cool, a police escort!" Wait 'til the guys see this pic!" A.J. said.

"Not exactly, but close enough," Sonia chuckled. "And around these parts, flashing lights is never a good thing."

Sonia's friend is one of the four NYPD officers who are stationed inside of Clinton during school hours. Sonia introduced A.J and Logan to Patrolman Erica Alvarado who had been stationed at the school for the last three years.

Erica opened the main student entrance as she was describing the way the school worked.

"When you get here, make sure you don't have anything which will make the metal detectors go off. Knives, things like that," Erica warned.

ZIP CODE

Why would anyone bring a knife to school? A.J. wondered to herself.

A.J. and Logan looked at the three detectors and were literally dumbfounded. They said nothing. They looked at each other in a way which said, *holy crap, what did we sign up for?*

"Your cell phones will be taken..." Erica said.

"What?!!" They didn't mean to be rude and interrupt but, A.J. and Logan both burst out the same word at the same time.

Erica continued and they knew she meant it..."and placed in a bag, with your student number and name. When the session ends, you go to the cafeteria and reclaim your property," Erica said.

"No cell phones at all during the day? Not even lunch?" Logan asked.

"Correct, no cell phones permitted during the school day," Erica said in an admonishing tone.

"What about our Apple I-books?" A.J. asked.

"Your what?" Erica asked.

Our I-Books, a laptop," Logan said.

"I don't think that will be a problem in the Einstein Program, but you will have to ask tomorrow," Erica said.

"So not every student is given a laptop when the come to school?" A.J. asked.

"Hell, no."

Logan and A.J. glanced at each other again. *Is this a school or a jail?* A.J though to herself.

How do they do any research or play a game during study hall? Logan thought.

Ericka took them on a quick tour of the building. The tour took the New Jersey bumpkins past the main office, into the cafeteria, the library, and then up the third floor where the Einstein Program held classes, and finally the massive gymnasium.

"May I ask a silly question? Please don't take this wrong, but what are the biggest problems the students have here at Clinton?" A.J. asked.

"I'm glad you aksed dat," Erica said in her pronounced Latina-Bronx accent. "Robbery and fighting." A.J. and Logan looked at each other again. This time they looked right into each other's eyes and held the look.

A.J. mouthed the words, *"Holy shit!"*

"Keep your valuables close to you; don't leave your purse or wallet out of your possession for five seconds. Absolutely walk away from knuckleheads who start any shit in the hallways. There is very little fighting in the Einstein Program, so I wouldn't be too concerned about that if I were you. The Einstein and Macy kids are really serious about their work. On the second floor? Not so much," Ericka said.

CHAPTER 6

The New York Botanical Garden in the Bronx is a glorious place. Twenty-eight specialty gardens including an authentic and fabulous, Japanese garden are some of the reasons why so many schools and families visit all year round.

During the holiday season, from late November until mid-January, the Train Show is an amazing display of one hundred and fifty landmarks including The Brooklyn Bridge, The Statue of Liberty, and Rockefeller Center. Each location is recreated with natural materials like tree bark, leaves, and grass. At the end of a half-mile of train tracks, a wonderful finalé of sound and light captivates the visitors.

Sonia didn't have to pay the twenty-dollar All-Garden Pass fee for her or the thirty-six dollar entrance tickets for A.J. and Logan. Sometimes being a police officer and knowing the head of security paid off.

The three of them stayed until six in the evening and really enjoyed themselves.

Logan and A.J. took a dozen selfies at the Botanical Gardens, sending them via Instagram, Facebook and Snapchat to their friends with various subtitles; IN THE BOOGY DOWN BOTANICAL GARDENS; Amazing train show...beats Thomas the Train to shit; Logan and Me at the BBG.

"I would never have guessed this place was in the middle of the Bronx. It's a treasure. I loved it!" A.J. declared.

"So why does the Bronx have such bad reputation?" Logan asked.

"Crime is one reason. Poverty is another. There is an awful lot of crime in the Bronx. Mostly drug related. Stealing, muggings, guns. That's why you need to keep your eyes and ears open. You must both look like you know your way around, otherwise you become an easy mark," Sonia said.

"So being white, we already stick out, right?" A.J. said.

"Don't get me wrong, there are plenty of white people who live in the Bronx, just not around where we live. Just be smart. Anyway, I want to treat you to a pizza on Arthur Avenue before we go home and get ready for tomorrow. We can walk there if you want," Sonia said.

"Sure, who doesn't like pizza?" Logan replied.

"You may find the pizza here is a bit different than you are used to in New Jersey...just sayin," Sonia said.

They walked along Fordham road toward Arthur Avenue.

"Right over there, behind those tall, black, wrought iron fences, is Fordham University. This is where Rosa will be attending school in August. She is so excited, and so am I. It's a dream come true for both of us." Sonia smiled broadly, with an obvious look of pride and satisfaction.

"Will she commute?" A.J. asked.

"She will live in that huge, freshman dorm we just passed. I had to pull some strings for that. Fordham is in high demand these days. Rosa got a full scholarship which includes living on campus. She wanted to have the full college experience. You know, not living with mommy any more. All Rosa has to do is keep her grades at a certain level. She will!"

"I hope to meet her one day," A.J. said.

"We can work on that. Right now, we are going to Giovanni's. I like them, and Full Moon's pizza is the best. Mario's is amazing, too, but it's a whole sit down dinner thing," Sonia said.

"I see a lot of...like... young people on this block," Logan said.

"They are mostly Fordham students. The University owns a lot of property on this strip of streets. The school uses them as off campus housing. You could say white kids, Logan. I won't be offended," Sonia stated.

"I was thinking just that, Sonia. I just didn't want it to come out wrong," Logan admitted.

"If there is one thing I would like the two of you to come away with, is that not every black and Latino are bad people. Like anywhere else, we have our share of loose marbles, but most of the people here are just trying to get by. It's not easy here, but it's not like being in hell either."

Sonia, A.J., and Logan approached East 187th Street. Even though it was chilly, the street was bustling with people. Parents with their college kids, couples going to their favorite, Italian restaurant or pizzeria, some locals sitting inside the pastry shops or hanging out on the sidewalks just people watching. A.J. was already getting smiles and winks from Latino men.

They arrived at Giovanni's and found an open table in the back of the restaurant.

"I haven't been to Ridgewood, but I'm going to bet you this pizza is nothing like you can get back home. You guys get to choose the toppings," Sonia said.

A waitress came over to their table, pad ready in hand. She was chewing and snapping her gum. "What can I get yas?"

"A pizza. Is pepperoni and sausage okay with you guys?" Logan asked Sonia and A.J.

"Fine by me," Sonia said.

"Can we add some mushrooms?" A. J. asked.

"Sure, large pie, sausage, pepperoni, and mushrooms. Drink?" the waitress asked.

"I'll have a Diet Coke," Sonia ordered.

"Regular Coke," Logan replied.

"Just water for me," A.J. said.

There was a paper place setting with a map of Italy showing all the regions and the special places of interest. A.J. wondered if this was a good place to visit in the summer before she began her freshman year at Brown.

Logan was on his cell answering messages.

ZIP CODE

Sonia let Logan and A.J. relax in their own worlds. A few minutes later, the waitress was back.

The steaming hot pizza arrived, as ordered, to the table. A.J. and Logan quickly took cell phone shots. Logan sent a group text:

> FORGET RENATO'S... This is REAL pizza

A.J. posted on Facebook for her eleven hundred and twelve friends to see and a personal text to her parents:

> MAMA MIA... It tastes as good as it looks. At Giovanni's in THE BRONX

They gobbled up the pizza pie. A.J. was licking the oil from her fingers.

"Not even close!" Logan announced.

"What's that, Logan?" Sonia asked.

"Ridgewood pizza. Not even close to this. Amazing!" Logan said.

"I need to pace myself with the food here. First the great eggs and rice, now this pizza! Oh my God!" A.J. exclaimed.

"You have heard of the freshman fifteen, right? Those extra pounds know no race. Now we go around the corner for a cannoli, and then a Gypsy cab back to *mi casa*," Sonia said.

ZIP CODE

Sonia paid the bill and the three walked out of Giovanni's and made a left toward De Lillo Pastry Shop. They walked a few feet and a man stopped A.J. He was short, wearing a tattered, New York Yankee hat, and had very large ears. His mouth was open, his misaligned teeth, and a protruding, lower lip conveyed he was mentally challenged.

"Hi, I missed you. Do you have some change?" the man asked.

"Sure, hold on a sec," A.J. said. They man came closer to her. Sonia and Logan stood there watching the transaction.

A.J. lowered the strap from her shoulder and opened her purse. She took out a dollar and gave it to the unfortunate panhandler. Logan took a quick photo.

"Thank-you, pretty lady," the man said, then quickly walked away.

A.J. turned back to a smiling Sonia and Logan.

"Logan, if you post that and my parents see it, I'm toast!" A.J. warned.

"Dude, I gotcha. No worries," Logan replied.

"That was very nice of you, A.J. and a good segue for a lesson. If you plan on giving money to every street panhandler in the Bronx, you are going to need lots of money. If you must, just keep a few coins in your pocket and move away quickly. Never, ever open your purse and fish out money like that. That poor soul was innocent but the next guy or woman can grab your purse, knock you to the ground, and you will watch his smoke as he flees with your money, your ID, driver's license, and credit cards. Understood?" Sonia asked.

"I guess that is what street smarts is all about," A.J. sheepishly said.

"It's a beginning, sweetie," Sonia said.

"So we just walk on by without any contact, I guess," Logan said.

"Now you got it!" Sonia said.

The cannoli was insane, the cappuccino was an experience, and the cab ride back home was an adventure.

A.J. and Logan were ready for the first day at DeWitt Clinton High School the next morning.

At least they thought they were.

CHAPTER 7

Rosa looked out of her bedroom window just as the sun was coming up. She hardly slept due to the anticipation of starting her first day at Ridgewood High.

Rosa stared at the light mist of heat coming off the Olympic size, in-ground pool. The pool was dwarfed by the four-acre back yard, surrounded by thick woods. Various birds were searching for their breakfast; two Blue Jays flew around a bramble patch, facing off for a fight. A plump, red Robin was preening itself in the bronze birdbath. Rabbits and squirrels were beginning their day just as Rosa was.

The view was a far cry from Rosa's bedroom facing Fox Street in the Bronx. A corner Bodega with a twelve-foot high, graffiti covered wall, an empty lot, and a newly renovated four- story, red brick building was etched into Rosa's memory.

Semaj's alarm clock went off thirty minutes later. He slept like a baby. Just as he did before every bedtime at home, Semaj said the prayers his mom and he recited together. He prayed for his Lord and Savior, Jesus Christ to protect him and make him learn the most he could in school. The prayers brought great comfort to Semaj, and helped to give him the confidence he needed to succeed.

Semaj and Rosa planned to go downstairs to the kitchen together. Rosa tapped lightly on Semaj's bedroom door. Semaj was just finishing brushing his teeth and grunted a "give me a second" response. The two, new, Ridgewood seniors followed the smell of coffee and waffles to their destination.

"Good morning, guys. Sleep well?" Mrs. Taylor asked.

"Fabulous, and those waffles smell amazing," Semaj said.

"Not so good. I mean the bed is soooo comfortable but I think I'm just very nervous," Rosa admitted.

"Oh, that's natural, Rosa. Just have a good breakfast and I'll run you over to the school."

"I'm not sure I can hold anything down," Rosa said. She held both hands against her stomach.

"Try some fruit and yogurt, or some oatmeal. That will coat your stomach," Mrs. Taylor prescribed.

A.J. and Semaj looked at each other in amazement over the selection which was spread out on the kitchen's green and beige, granite, center island.

"Do you prepare a spread like this every morning, Mrs. Taylor? Semaj asked.

"Give or take. Mr. Taylor enjoys a hearty breakfast. His driver takes him to the city early. He works out at the club, and then has a mid-morning snack. Some days he just grabs some coffee and toast, and a hard-boiled egg and starts his day lighter."

"I would be as big as a house," Rosa said.

ZIP CODE

Semaj put two waffles with butter and syrup and some fresh fruit on his plate, and moved to the round, glass kitchen table. He poured a large glass of orange juice.

"We could discuss nutrition at some point, Rosa. I have a Masters Degree in Nutrition from Rutgers."

"I would love that. I've been a bit chubby my entire life. I think I'll take your advice and try the yogurt," Rosa said.

"Try that granola too. You will be amazed how it will keep you satisfied all morning. By the way, the lunch at the school is wonderful. I was involved with planning the menu, along with the school nutritionist and chef. Semaj, you can eat slower, we have plenty of time."

"Sorry, it's a bad habit. It's so good, though." Semaj held his hand in front of his face to avoid talking with a mouth full of food.

Mrs. Taylor sat at the table giving last-minute instructions to Rosa and Semaj. They were to report to a guidance counselor who would get them to their homeroom class and review their schedule and also give them a map of their classes. They would be picked up at two forty-five by Mrs. Taylor at the East Ridgewood Avenue circle inside the campus. They should say hello to Mrs. Guardino, the schools librarian, and give her Mrs. Taylor's best regards.

Ten minutes later, Semaj in his new Ridgewood hoodie, and Rosa wearing her best distressed jeans and a shirred, long sleeve blouse which draped down past her midriff, both hopped into Mrs. Taylor's Range Rover for the five-minute ride to their new school.

Rosa's stomach went into a knot as they arrived at the circle. She tried to take a selfie, but her hands were shaking too badly.

When they left the SUV, Semaj pulled Rosa close to him and took a selfie in front of the Ridgewood High School letters on the brick wall near the student entrance. Semaj posted the photo on Facebook and on Snapchat:

> BRAVE NEW WORLD...
> wish us luck!

He tagged Rosa Colon for Facebook and posted to his story on Snapchat.

Semaj said a quick, silent prayer to his Lord and Savior.

CHAPTER 8

A.J. Taylor had a restless night. She tossed and turned and just couldn't fall into a deep sleep. The day on the train, at the Botanical Gardens, Giovanni's pizza shop, and the poor-soul panhandler kept replaying in her mind.

At three o'clock in the morning, A.J. needed to use the bathroom and found her way through the chilly apartment. She flipped on the light in the small bathroom and saw spots. Well, at first she thought they were spots. Instead, they were cockroaches which fled to safety under the old, four-legged, bathtub legs and into the white, metal cabinet under the sink. One, large roach went directly toward A.J.'s bare feet sending her jumping out of its way. She fled for the relative safety of her bedroom. A.J. went right to her cell phone and pounded out a text to her best friend Erin Gallagher.

EG...what did I get myself into? They have cockroaches. Big, brown monsters that run at the sight of light and humans. Holy crap! What if they get into my bed? EWWWWWW!!!

At 3 A.M., no response came from the sound asleep Erin, tucked warmly into her bed, nineteen miles away in virtually cockroach-free Ridgewood, New Jersey.

A.J. sat in her bed, put her slippers on and vowed never to walk without them again. She waited for the sun to come up, wondering how her first day at Clinton would be without a good night's sleep.

At that hour of the morning, from her bedroom window, the Bronx seemed serene, almost beautiful, with all of the different-looking buildings reflecting the early morning sun. A couple of mangy, stray dogs trotted down the middle of Fox Street, both pulling on the same white and blue White Castle, hamburger bag.

Logan slept like a log. Before he went to sleep, Logan, as he did every night at home, did deep breathing and Yoga stretching exercises to help break the anxiety he felt before a day of school.

The pressure of achieving the great grades he was expected to deliver was enormous. Especially because Logan was not a naturally-gifted student. He had to work exceptionally hard to keep up with the other honors students at Ridgewood. This day would have its own variety of stress, and the exercises were Logan's way of dealing with pressure. Some of his friends used drugs for that. Prescription and illegal.

He woke about thirty minutes after daylight to the sound of the repetitive, beating, Latin music from the downstairs neighbors. He heard the shower running in the bathroom which was right outside his tiny bedroom. He imagined A.J. taking a shower and pushed the image out of his mind.

Sonia worked the eight to twelve shift at the precinct, so she didn't have to get up until around six forty-five. She was not planning on waking early to see Logan and A.J. out the door at six-thirty. Sonia gave them adequate directions on how to get to the subway station. Both A.J. and Logan put the train directions and schedule into their cell phones. A bagel store, and a Dunkin' Donuts on the way to the Cypress Avenue station was a sufficient breakfast. Logan and A.J. needed to be at school by eight o'clock, so they would have plenty of time to get to Clinton, even if there was a train delay.

The walk to the subway was uneventful. The streets are quiet at that time in the morning. The Jersey kids picked up a buttered bagel and a medium container of Tropicana orange juice. They would have plenty of time to eat their meal on the train.

The smell of urine on the steps leading down into the subway turned A.J.'s stomach which was already doing backflips. Logan put his nose next to his armpit just to make sure the smell wasn't coming from him.

A.J. wore a pair of black leggings under a short denim skirt, a pair of brown Uggs, a bulky, white, Irish Aran sweater, and a light, ski jacket. Logan wore his maroon and black Ridgewood Crew jacket, jeans, and a pair of Air Jordan 1, gray, hi-top sneakers.

To say A. J. and Logan stuck out like sore thumbs would be just about right. The preppy look they both carried was as if they were wearing a sign saying, *We are rich kids from New Jersey, or Westchester, or some other place where money is plentiful.* As if being white wasn't enough.

The train ride up to Harlem was half-empty. A.J. and Logan grabbed the first seats next to the door and opened their brown, paper bags to start eating their breakfasts.

As they began eating, A.J. looked up and noticed the other people on the train. It seemed everyone was staring at them. With her elbow, A.J. nudged Logan, his head still buried in his bagel. Logan followed her gaze toward the other commuters. He stopped chewing the doughy meal and looked around from person to person. A.J. took out her cellphone and double-checked the train directions. She just wanted to divert her eyes from the gaping onlookers. After a few seconds, Logan started looking up at the advertisements.

How rude can these people be? A.J. thought to herself.

Now I know how a hot chick in a bar feels, Logan said to himself.

The train rolled into the 125th Street Station in Harlem. Logan and A.J. followed the program and went downstairs to take the number four train back up to the Bronx. A second later, the train pulled up, and the doors were opened. The platform was crowded with high school and college students, everyone scampering for a seat. Logan pointed to a lone seat for A.J. to grab. He was okay standing over her, his long, muscular arms holding the high, vertical bar.

"Yo, wass up? Ha ya doin'?" A light-skinned, black guy with a short mane of dreadlocks asked A.J.

"I'm fine, thank-you," A.J. replied. Twenty minutes into her first trip to school and she already made a mistake.

"I know you fine. Das why I chat you up."

"Yo, she's with me," Logan said. Confrontation may not have been the best tactic, but Logan felt he had to protect his friend.

"Is cool, my nigga," Dreadlocks said. He took his attention elsewhere on the train.

ZIP CODE

"Alexandra, do me a favor. Don't respond to that kind of thing. Just ignore them and look away, okay?" Logan admonished.

"I get it, Loge. I need to journal this one when I get home tonight. First the roaches, now this guy. I'm learning quickly," A.J. said.

"Roaches? What Roaches?" Logan asked.

"Sonia's apartment has roaches. One nearly attacked me in the bathroom this morning. I held in a pee for like two hours," A.J. whispered.

Logan laughed so loud some of the other riders seemed to wake from their semi-conscious state.

"They don't attack people, A.J. Just stomp them," Logan advised.

"No way am I stomping those ugly suckers in my bare feet... just no way," A.J. said.

The two, Ridgewood High transfer students both laughed out loud. The laugh broke their tension, and they started to be themselves, loose and animated with each other as if they were together at the Garden State Plaza Mall back in New Jersey.

A short time later, the train pulled into the Mosholu Parkway/Jerome Avenue Station. The train, filled with black, Hispanic, Indian, and Asian students funneled through the open train doors, all heading to the long set of stairs which led to Jerome Ave- nue.

Logan pointed to DeWitt Clinton High School. They made it in one piece.

CHAPTER 9

A.J. and Logan walked with the crowd of students toward Clinton. A group of Asian and Indian students veered off to the left and onto the Bronx Science campus, behind Clinton. Almost everyone wore a backpack to carry his or her books. A few girls had larger shoulder bags for the same purpose.

More than half of the kids, both Clinton and Bronx Science wore ear buds, listening to their own favorite music. Most of the Clinton boys wore hoodie jackets, but only a few carried backpacks. Anyone who carried books at Clinton are Macy or Einstein students. These are the students who are serious about their educations. They were not just marking time.

Walking along West Mosholu Parkway, A.J. and Logan looked out of place to say the very least. The only white kids walking among a sea of brown and blacks, the two Ridgewood students looked as if they were beamed down from the Starship Enterprise onto an alien planet.

Suddenly, just before the entrance to the school, there was an argument involving several of the students, both male and female. A.J. and Logan changed their direction to avoid the tumult.

A young, Hispanic boy, short, stocky, and dark, with his face covered by a hoodie, without warning, ran up upon a tall, thin, black student, and seemingly punched him in his lower midsection. The black kid fell onto the short grass, and rolled onto a patch of hard, brown dirt.

The Hispanic boy ran back toward the train station. Screams from the small crowd erupted as two of the downed student's friends quickly moved to help him.

"This isn't what I expected on day one," Logan said.

"That must have been a lucky punch. The guy went down pretty fast," A.J. stated.

"C'mon, not our business. Let's just get inside," Logan advised.

The sound of a police siren from a few blocks away grew closer by the second. A female police officer ran from the school to the growing crowd around the tall, black kid. The cop was speaking into her two-way radio attached to the right lapel on her uniform.

A.J. turned at the steps of the school for a final look at the scene, the crowd shielding the scene. Logan gently grabbed A.J. by her jacket sleeve, and they were inside the school.

For the first time in their three and a half years of secondary education, Logan and A.J. passed through a metal detector to enter school. Once inside, their cell phones were taken by a security guard and placed into a bag, their names and student ID numbers written on the outside and stapled shut. They would retrieve their phones at the end of the day.

A.J. looked at Logan and said, "I already feel naked and afraid. This is the first time since fifth grade I've been without my phone. How will I survive for seven hours?"

Suddenly, a large, heavy-set Hispanic man, another man and a woman, who both looked like teachers, rushed past the entering students to attend to the situation in front of the school.

"Clear the way please; step to the side," Mr. Taveleres shouted. "Move, please. Let's go! Move away from the door," the male teacher shouted.

Students crowded against the wall nearest to the metal detectors. The security officer made sure no student entered on either side of the detectors.

A.J. and Logan were standing in the marble rotunda, inside the school, both a bit confused at the mayhem which ensued.

If my mom saw this, I would be back in Ridgewood in twenty minutes, A.J. thought to herself.

As the chaos continued, a short, well-dressed woman walked in front of A.J. and Logan.

"Alexandra and Logan, I assume? I'm Ms. Romeo. I'm the head of guidance for the Einstein Program. Welcome to DeWitt Clinton."

"Hi, Miss Romeo. Nice to meet you." A.J. forced a smile.

"A little, early morning scuffle outside," Logan added.

"Mr. Taveleres just passed you. He wanted to welcome you both as well, but he's very hands-on when it comes to student conflicts. I suppose he will see you later in the day. Let's go up to the third floor and get to your homeroom class. We have a few minutes to review your schedule and go over your classroom assignments," Ms. Romeo said. Eva Romeo looked too young to be a guidance counselor. Her thick, Bronx accent did not go with her angelic face and athletic figure. She was all business. *She doesn't look like she will take any shit from anyone,* Logan thought to himself.

Ms. Romeo walked quickly and kept ahead of the two Ridgewood, transfer students. As she spoke with them about school logistics, Ms. Romeo would occasionally glance back at Logan and A.J. to check their attention and interest.

The clean, buffed, tiled floors, ultra-high ceilings and old, wooden, school room doors were a blur as Ms. Romeo went on about the Einstein Program and the success of last year's students. A.J. and Logan's destination was room 302, their designated homeroom.

After a brief review of courses and classrooms, Ms. Romeo wished the Jersey kids the best of luck and got back on her fast horse.

"Hi, I'm Luie Morales. Welcome to Clinton and Einstein. Nice to meet you." Luie shook Logan's and A.J.'s hands with both of his.

Luie Morales is a Puerto Rican with something to prove. Light skinned and ruggedly handsome, Luie spent a few months in Spofford Juvenile Center in the South Bronx when he was thirteen years old. That year, the notorious, vermin infested Spofford was finally closed due to abuse and violence. Luie got a small taste of incarceration at Spofford, and vowed to himself and his parents to change his delinquent ways. His goal is to be a lawyer. Luie's ninety-six percent average is his proud, badge of honor.

"Nice meeting you, Luie. I'm glad someone broke the ice and said hello. Coming to a new school as a last semester senior is worse than my first day at middle school," A.J. said with a beaming smile.

"I guess we were baptized with our first, Bronx fight this morning," Logan noted.

"Yeah, I'm sorry for that. There are a lot of fights around here. Evidently, it wasn't a student who stabbed that kid. It was some gang-banger from Kelly Towers next door. So foolish," Luie said. He closed his eyes, pursed his lips and shook his head to the negative.

"Stabbed! That boy was actually stabbed?" A.J. uttered.

"It looked to us like he just punched him in the stomach," Logan added.

"He was stabbed alright. I heard he's going to be all right though, thank God. Here, let me introduce you to everyone."

A.J. and Logan looked at each other in total disbelief. A.J. felt as if she needed to sit down. Logan thought to himself, *Welcome to the jungle, asshole.*

LOUIS ROMANO

CHAPTER 10

07045

Ridgewood High School

Where are the security guards? The metal detectors? Semaj thought to himself. He and Rosa walked down the spotless hallway toward the principal's office as they were instructed to do on their first day at Ridgewood High.

"Well this has a different feel. It's more like I imagine college is like. Look at this place. It's so much different than Clinton. Like a different world entirely. Everyone is loose. The hallways seem much smaller. And we get to keep our phones with us all day!" Rosa exclaimed.

"And clean. I don't see papers all over the floors, and the bulletin boards aren't all torn up like at Clinton. I guess they don't have any Spanish people here," Semaj said. He didn't realize what his comment sounded like to Rosa.

"Dude, what is that supposed to mean?" Rosa asked.

"No offense, Rosa, but I see a lot of Hispanics just throw candy wrappers and other stuff right on the floor instead of dumping waste in a garbage pail. I see it in the streets all the time," Semaj said.

"Oh, so blacks are neat freaks, I suppose. That is such a bigoted statement. I'm surprised at you," Rosa scolded.

"Just my observations, that's all. Just being honest."

"And I see blacks throwing chicken bones and watermelon rinds all over the place. How do you like that statement?" Rosa asked. *Stupid douche,* Rosa thought.

"Okay, sorry. I guess you're right. I apologize. Look, we are way in the minority here. We have to stick together."

"No worries. Sorry if I was overly sensitive. I'm just nervous," Rosa said. She felt badly about jumping on her only friend at the moment.

Entering the main office, Rosa and Semaj were met by an older woman who sat at her desk next to the office entrance.

"Hello. Welcome to Ridgewood High. I'm Madeline Atwell, I'm Doctor Connelly's Administrative Assistant." Mrs. Atwell looked like Robin Williams in *Mrs. Doubtfire.*

"I'm Rosa Colon, very nice to meet you Mrs. Atwell." Rosa's voice betrayed her nervousness.

"And I'm Semaj Henry. So happy to be here! You have a beautiful school."

"Why, thank you very much. We do our best. Doctor Connelly is at a principal's conference in Trenton, but Mr. Spechler will officially welcome you. He should be in his homeroom. First, let me give you each your Chromebooks. You will find your schedules on the special icon. I'm certain the uploaded software will be sufficient to get you started. Let's go see if Mr. Spechler is upstairs."

As they walked up the stairway to the second floor, most everyone they passed or walked next to seemed friendly. A few students said hi, some smiled. A woman stopped and introduced herself as Rosa and Semaj's Calculus teacher. She shook both of their hands firmly and seemed very nice.

As they turned onto the second floor from the stairwell, there was a banner which draped from above the classroom doors, across the hallway.

RHS WELCOMES ROSA AND SEMAJ
DEWITT CLINTON CLASS OF 2015.

Rosa smiled widely and Semaj laughed out loud.

Suddenly, Rosa's apprehension disappeared. She felt welcome. *Never expected this kind of greeting. This is so thoughtful,* Rosa thought.

Ron Spechler was waiting for them at the entrance to his classroom; his broad smile and welcoming face made Semaj and Rosa's spirits soar.

"The day has finally arrived. Hi, I'm Mr. Spechler. This is such an honor for me." He greeted Rosa first and then Semaj, shaking their hands firmly with a sincerely, warm greeting.

"Come on in and meet your classmates. They assembled here to greet you. Then I'll go over your schedules and class assignments," Spechler said.

The large classroom was filled to standing room only. As Semaj and Rosa entered, some of their fellow seniors clapped. A few whistled like they were at a Maroons basketball game. There were dozens of homemade maroon and black cupcakes on Spechler's desk, made by the moms in the Ridgewood High School Parent's Club.

"Okay, let's settle down, people. It is my great pleasure to introduce to you all, Rosa Colon and Semaj Henry…honors seniors from DeWitt Clinton High School in the Bronx. They will be your classmates for your final semester. Rosa and Semaj are part the program our A.J. Taylor and Logan Darby are attending at their school. This had been a dream of mine for some time, and I'm delighted to have these two, very bright students with us. We have some time set aside for everyone to mingle and get to know each other. Please make them feel at home," Spechler announced.

Another round of applause and whistles ensued. A few of the jocks swaggered up to the desk for the sweets. Rosa and Semaj found themselves enveloped by their new classmates.

Holy crap. I wonder if anyone is doing this for the two, new kids at Clinton. I would bet dollars to cupcakes that's not happening, Semaj thought.

CHAPTER 11

BACK AT 10468

DEWITT CLINTON

The school day was uneventful. A.J. was asked to hang out with two tough guys from the second floor. One guy was black. A.J. really didn't see color, but she didn't care for a few of the things he said to her. A Dominican guy seemed nice enough, except the tattoos going up on either side of his neck indicated he was a bit more worldly for her at the moment.

After their last class, Logan and A.J. headed down the three flights of stairs to retrieve their cell phones in the school's cafeteria.

"Jesus, I can't wait to get on Snapchat. I feel like an addict who needs a fix. How did we live before cellphones? I must have three hundred messages, and I have no idea how many Facebook hits I have waiting," A.J. said.

"Did you notice anything today, except no cell phones?" Logan asked.

"That I'm very popular among the guys? Walking in the halls, I felt like I was being undressed. And that Latino kissy thing... yuck!"

"No, I mean about the classes."

"No, what?" A.J. asked.

"They are doing work we did like sophomore year. Especially in math and chem."

"Yes, I noticed. The kids are really paying attention and trying hard, though. The teachers are really, really dedicated to the students. It's nothing like I imagined. I thought the kids would be more disruptive. I don't know, maybe more inattentive."

"And I got digits from three of the ladies from the second floor. Two just put them in my hand. One asked me for my cell number so she could text me," Logan said, with a slight sense of pride.

"Did you give it her?"

"Of course. Why not? I'm a free agent!" Logan exclaimed.

"Just be careful, Pappi...I thought I heard one girl call you Pappi. I almost threw up in my mouth," A.J. said, pretending to put her finger down her throat.

The two Jersey kids waited on a short line for their cell phones. A.J. snapped it out of the security officers hand a bit to anxiously. The officer flashed a dirty look.

As they headed for the Jerome Avenue El, A.J. and Logan ignored everything around them, and began pounding the keys on their phones.

First day of school in the Bronx, and there is a stabbing outside the school. Plus I got hit on like a pole dancer. Begging no one tell my mom. A.J. posted to her story on Snapchat.

ZIP CODE

The replies came back in droves.

"WTF A.J. get on the first bus back here. Miss you!"
"That's insane! Did the dude die?"
"So it's not just good pizza?"
"I'm praying for you A.J. Go with the Lord."
"I would have wet myself."

Logan texted his group:

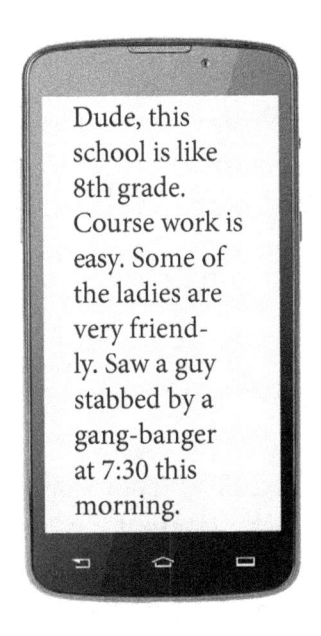

> Dude, this school is like 8th grade. Course work is easy. Some of the ladies are very friendly. Saw a guy stabbed by a gang-banger at 7:30 this morning.

His phone lit up with responses.

"Tell me more about the ladies, bro!!!"
"Crips and Bloods?"

"Did he buy the farm???"
"Watch your butt, whitey."

The train was less crowed on the way back to Fox Street. Mostly students from the surrounding schools and a few seedy, street people in various stages of consciousness."

"Loge...look at the guy over there. He's leaning over standing in the middle of the train. How is he still standing on a moving train?" A.J. asked.

"He's a junkie. Probably heroin. I saw this in a movie once. He has no idea where he is."

"Oh...my...God. A real, live, heroin junkie?"

"In the flesh. Bet you a coke he doesn't fall down."

"No way, I can't even bear to look. Incredibly sad," A.J. said, tears welling in her eyes.

The transfer at 125th Street was also fairly empty. Other than some Asians, mostly students, A.J. and Logan were the only people not of color on both trains. Except for a very dirty, smelly, white lady, who pulled a flimsy, old, shopping cart behind her. She talked out loud to herself on the entire trip back up to the Bronx.

For a chilly afternoon, the streets were bustling with people. Loud, Latin music beat through the air with a syncopated rhythm. A block away, a hip-hop hit blared from a discount variety store. The music started people waving their arms and hands to the beat. The pungent aroma of fried *Cuchifritos,* mostly made of pork, caught the afternoon breeze and permeated the entire block. *I am going to ralph for sure,* Logan thought.

"What is that smell? It smells like burning cats," A.J. blurted.

Two blocks away, just as the fried pork left their sinuses, A.J and Logan passed *Wong's Sabor Kitchen Comidas Chino e Latinas Cuisine.*

"Now that smells pretty good. Is it Chinese or Spanish?" A.J. said.

"Read the sign, A.J. It's both. Want an egg roll?" Logan asked.

"Sure, but that front window looks like it hasn't been cleaned in about two years."

The gringo and the gringa went into Wong's and stepped up to the worn, plastic-topped counter. The Chinese lady behind the counter stared at them as if she just saw Mao Zedong walk into her shop.

Logan ordered the two egg rolls. The lady never looked away from the white, Jersey kids as she stuffed the greasy tubes into a brown, paper bag. Logan paid the staring woman and took a handful of napkins from the counter-top.

This is going to make me crap for days. If my mother could see me now, Logan thought.

A.J. took a bite of the egg roll, the hot oil dripping through the napkin and onto her hand.

"It's delicious. A little greasy, but very tasty," A.J. announced.

Logan bit into his snack; the hot oil from the eggroll scorched his lip and tongue.

"Wow, is that hot. Jeez, I may never feel my lips again."

Logan managed to inhale some cold air to mix with the fried, Chinese wrapper shell with bits of pork and vegetables.

"That is very good!" Logan said, still sucking in the air to cool off the food in his mouth.

"Yo, yo, blondie, *que pasa*? You need a ride, mommie?" The driver of a filthy, white van shouted out to A.J. from across the street. His partner in the driver's seat leaned over and said something indistinguishable in Spanish.

Logan started to give the middle finger when at the last second he remembered where he was. A.J. recalled what Sonia had said to her. She kept her gaze forward as if the two idiots in the van didn't exist. A.J. and Logan walked on...no harm, no foul.

A.J.'s cell phone rang. It was her mom calling.

"Hi, Mom."

"Alexandra, I heard what happened this morning. My heart is in my mouth. When daddy gets home, we are coming to get you."

"Mom, nothing happened. There was a fight which involved a local guy and a student. It had nothing to do with us. Logan and I were nowhere near that, so stop worrying. I'm fine."

"When Erica called, I almost fainted."

ZIP CODE

That friggin' BITCH! A.J. thought.

"Oh mom, she is just a gossip. Look, we are just walking home. It's a beautiful day here. Everything is fine. I'll call you after dinner, okay?"

A.J. successfully calmed her mom down, and they said their goodbyes.

"That witch-face Erica told my mom about the stabbing. I absolutely loathe her. And she pretends to be a friend," A.J. seethed.

"So why do you have her on your chat list?" Logan asked.

"Because she is the vice-president of the student council, and I don't want her to think I hate her. You know, keep your enemies closer thing."

"Why don't you two get along?"

"It's a long story. Roger asked me to Junior Prom. I said yes. She had a crush on him. High girly drama. Since then it's been very cool. And now this stunt."

"Let's be careful what we post going forward. My mom and dad will freak if they hear about the stabbing," Logan said.

"Agreed. Our weekly report to Mr. Spechler will be from our journals. We will just keep the chat general," A.J. advised.

"Let's get home. I'm looking forward to seeing what Sonia is making for dinner.

CHAPTER 12

10455

Fox Street, Bronx, NY

"I came home early this afternoon to make you guys a special dinner. You are in for a special meal, my lovelies. I'm not one to get up to make breakfast, but here you are; *Arroz con gandules y pernil.* The only way roast pork should be served. I assumed neither of you are Muslims," Sonia laughed.

"Dude, that smells delicious," Logan said.

The three of them sat at the small kitchen table. Sonia served the moist *pernil* with a large scoop of *gandules,* pigeon peas with yellow rice.

A.J. spotted a cockroach which scampered from the bottom of the stove to safety under the refrigerator.

Mother of God, how can I eat now? She said. Bile ran from her stomach into her throat.

"That is seriously spicy," Logan said.

"It's spiced with *Sofrito.* No good Puerto Rican cooks without it," Sonia declared.

A.J. put the roach out her mind and tasted the spicy dish.

"So did you guys see that knucklehead stab the student today?" Sonia asked.

"Yes. We though he just punched the kid. We didn't hang around to see the rest. We just went right inside the school," A.J. said.

"It was amazing. The dude just ran up to the black kid and wham, he punched him, or stabbed him right in the stomach and the kid went down," Logan added.

"Then the short guy started running, and everyone was yelling and screaming. It was bad," A.J. explained.

"Yeah, then the principal..."

"Okay, take it easy you two. It's good you went into the school. That was a smart thing to do. I heard about the incident and made a few calls. The student and the perp were in a drug deal that went bad. The victim will be okay. Luckily it wasn't a deep wound. We know who the perp is. He's a real *puñeta*. Just a day or two and he'll be apprehended. Unless he goes on the lamb," Sonia stated.

"What's a *puñeta*?" Logan asked.

"Not a very nice word. Like a jerkoff," Sonia laughed.

"Oh, we have some *puñeta's* in Ridgewood," Logan said.

"Yeah, one is Erica," A.J. added.

"What's that about?" Sonia asked.

ZIP CODE

"This girl at school. I think a better word is bitch. She told my mom about the stabbing. Mom went ballistic."

"I know. Your mom called me today. I calmed her down a bit. What happened today doesn't happen very often at Clinton. She's okay right now. Just keep your wits about you," Sonia said.

It got dark early, so A.J. and Logan decided to stay home that night, watching television, listening to their music, and texting their friends.

Logan received a surprise from the girl who took his cell phone number. She sent a selfie with she and her girlfriend, a suggestive photo of her in a bikini. Naturally, like all males of that age, Logan sent the photo to his chat group. Responses came in quickly:

"I'm in love!"
"Does she have a sister, Logan?"
"Look at that butt! She looks like JLo."
"Careful tiger. She may have a boyfriend. I hear they are stabbing kids left and right at Clinton."

The banter went back and forth for hours. Logan responded with his own selfie back to the girl, Loida Milan, a senior, who was not in the Macy or Einstein Program. Loida and Logan traded texts for a while. They planned to meet on Saturday.

CHAPTER 13

07450

Ridgewood New Jersey

then to...

07652

Garden State Plaza Mall, Paramus, New Jersey

Mrs. Taylor picked Semaj and Rosa up at the end of their first day of school. Several seniors walked from the school with the two Bronxites. Semaj seemed popular with a few of the girls who scampered around frantically snapping selfies with the new senior as if he were a celebrity. Rosa was engrossed in a conversation with three, fellow, female seniors as well. Rosa's group seemed more serious...more tame.

Semaj and Rosa climbed up into the Range Rover to an excited Mrs. Taylor, who was quite chipper and cheery.

"Hi, you guys! How was the first day? Tell me everything."

"Really some nice people from the teachers, the students, everyone was so friendly. I love this place!" Semaj was exuberant.

"They had a banner, cupcakes, they made us feel like we were welcome. Even though we are very different," Rosa said.

"Different? Well, it's true we have only a few minority students at Ridgewood," Mrs. Taylor admitted.

"Not just our ethnic backgrounds. We are very different economically. We are different in so many ways, Mrs. Taylor. This is what the whole program is about. I suppose we will see how we can adapt to this way of life, and how the two Ridgewood kids at Clinton will deal with living with a lot less," Rosa said.

Mrs. Taylor didn't know how to respond to what she had just heard. She was taken aback by the matter-of-fact tone in Rosa's voice.

"Well, it's a learning experience for everyone. Mister Spechler is brilliant and very progressive. We have the utmost respect and admiration for him," Mrs. Taylor said.

This is going down a tough road, Semaj thought.

Semaj felt uneasy with the way the conversation was going. He decided to change the subject.

"One thing is for certain. These teachers give out a heavy load of homework. I think I need at least two full hours to wade through the reading and math," Semaj declared.

"Can't you see it, Semaj? Good grades and success are expected here. These kids are required to make something of themselves, where our students are not under that kind of daily pressure," Rosa said.

Oh God, she is sounding like a militant socialist. Shades of Che Guevara! Semaj pondered.

"Well Rosa, I...I'm not sure our students are actually required to get good grades. It's just that they may put pressure on themselves to get into good colleges. You know how competitive that is, right?" Mrs. Taylor asked.

Rosa didn't reply to the question. As they pulled up to *May as Well,* Rosa looked up at the magnificent home, feeling very small, intimidated, unworthy to be there. She had her doubts if this program would do anything to change how she was perceived in this world of affluence.

"So, I was thinking you guys could have a snack and relax a bit before dinner. You can do your homework now or tonight, whichever you prefer," Mrs. Taylor said.

"I'm doing my assignments now. Some people are picking me up after dinner to go to the mall and chill." Semaj announced,"

"That's wonderful, Semaj. How about you, Rosa?"

Rosa made a smarmy face and mouthed the words, *"some people"* toward Semaj before she answered Mrs. Taylor's question.

"I'm going to do my homework now, and relax tonight. I didn't get much sleep last night, so I'm probably going to bed early," Rosa said.

"Good choice. Dinner is at six fifteen. And Semaj, your curfew is at eleven. I have to run to the gym now, so you guys make yourselves at home." Mrs. Taylor opened a garage door with a remote. The door to the kitchen was always left unlocked. "By the way, the security code on the pad outside the garage is 1212 in case you ever need it," Mrs. Taylor added.

Some cut up fresh fruit, nuts, organic yogurt, freshly made peanut butter, and stone ground crackers were on the center island in the kitchen. A large bottle of Evian water, instead of soda, was the only beverage choice.

"Such a nice woman. So trusting to give us the security code, don't you think?" Semaj asked.

"Yeah, trusting. The minute we leave here and go back to the Bronx the code will be changed. Didn't you notice the security cameras around this place?" Rosa said.

"What's up with you, dude? You're like so foul for some reason. I can't believe your remark on how the kids here are expected to do well. That was a little out of line, Rosa," Semaj said. He smeared some peanut butter on a sliced apple.

"I feel so...I don't know...almost inferior to these kids. What's the point of this whole stupid experiment? To rub our noses in what we will never have?"

"Listen to me, Rosa Colon. Someone once said 'No one can make you feel inferior without your consent.' I think it was Eleanor Roosevelt. You have so much to offer. I know of another Puerto Rican girl from the Bronx who lived in the projects, whose mother was a single mom like yours, who didn't let anyone put her in a package. Supreme Court Justice Sonia Sotomayor, okay? So cut the bullshit and get the best out of this experience. Learn from it, and grow Rosa. And stop feeling sorry for yourself."

"Maybe your *certain people* make you feel like a big man, but you are just a sideshow for them, Semaj," Rosa spewed venomously at her Clinton friend.

ZIP CODE

"Why are you so jaded all of a sudden? Is it because I was invited and you weren't?" Semaj asked.

"If I'm being honest, yeah, maybe a little. I'll get over it," Rosa teared up.

Like someone was listening in, Rosa's cell phone rang. The sound of Latin drums were her ring alert.

"Hi ,it's Rosa...Hi, Melissa...sure...yeah, that sounds great... can you pick me up?....sure, seven is great...thanks Melissa, see you in a bit." Rosa's one-way conversation with her new, classmate friend was heaven sent.

"The Lord works in strange and mysterious ways. Thank-you, Jesus," Semaj said as he looked to the kitchen ceiling.

"I feel like such a shit now. I'm sorry, Semaj. I *was* feeling sorry for myself. You are a perfect friend. And nobody, no person is better than me, anywhere!" Rosa declared.

The two friends hugged. Then off they went to hit the books.

LOUIS ROMANO

CHAPTER 14

Worlds Collide

The school week went by quickly on both sides of the Hudson River. In New Jersey, Rosa and Semaj got a taste of the demanding workload the seniors were expected to accomplish at Ridgewood High. Conversely, A.J. and Logan found the curriculum and homework at DeWitt Clinton to be below what they experienced at their school.

Semaj and Rosa were enjoying the social life of Ridgewood; the mall, small gatherings at other students' lavish homes, the Starbucks, the Country Pancake House, Baumgarts Café, all along fancy East Ridgewood Avenue. A.J. and Logan didn't stray too far from Sonia's small, Fox Street apartment.

That was to change on their first Saturday living in the Bronx. A few of the Clinton students invited the Ridgewood kids to meet them at the "Hub" at eight in the evening.

Saturday morning found A.J. and Logan having *Café Bustelo* coffee, and getting ready to take an afternoon walking around the area. Sonia was working, and had left the apartment early. Or so she said in a text message to Logan and A.J. Logan surmised she had a date. A.J. said she never heard her come home last night.

It was a sunny, but crisp, morning without a cloud in the sky. A.J. and Logan were also going to take a bus back to Arthur Avenue for some more pizza and Italian pastries.

"I Googled The Hub last night. Sounds amazing, Logan! It's not far from here. East 149th Street, or as they say around here 'a hun forty-ninth.' So it's where Willis, Melrose, and Third Avenues all meet. Get this! The Hub is the second busiest place in New York City after Times Square. One hundred and fifty-four thousand people live in the area surrounding The Hub. The entire town of Ridgewood, New Jersey has roughly twenty-five thousand residents...that's wild!" A.J. said.

"You mean 'a hun forty ninfe street.' Really...someone has to teach these kids to speak English. I caught myself yesterday saying *axed* instead of *asked*," Logan added.

"Really, Logan? Really? They don't all speak like that."

"Wow, I sound like my parents, don't I? That's so bigoted. I guess I'm just conditioned. Most of these kids are really nice. I'm sorry I said that, A.J."

"I'm conditioned, too. My dad is pretty liberal, but my mom is right out of Attila the Hun. This guy asked me out for tonight. His name is Keith. Do you know him? Keith Copeland?" A.J. asked.

"Yeah, he's that black kid with the mini-fro."

"That's him."

"So what did you say?" Logan asked.

"I didn't say yes or no. I told him you and I were going to The Hub tonight to meet some people, and he said he would check it out too."

"So, big deal?"

"Big deal? My mom would probably kill me and then slit her wrists if I dated a black," A.J. whispered. As if someone in the apartment could hear.

"My parents would freak, too. But how do you feel about it, A.J.?" Logan also whispered.

"I'm okay with it. Keith is a really nice guy. He's an honors student, he's certainly very good looking, and I like him as a friend. So what's the big deal?"

"Just asking. Look. I think my parents would freak if they found out I'm meeting a Dominican girl tonight," Logan said.

"Oh, so it's a date with you and that Loida?"

"I guess you can call it a date. We're all meeting at that hip hop place. Not actually a date where we are going together alone somewhere."

"She seems to hang with a rougher crowd than the Macy and Einstein kids," A.J. noted.

"Yeah, but she has that great J-Lo butt, an' shit," Logan joked. He mimicked a Latino accent.

"Ewwww!" A.J. pretended to gag.

The Ridgewood kids explored the streets surrounding their neighborhood. Nothing much was going on, so they decided to get to the Italian enclave of Arthur Avenue as planned.

The streets were busy with shoppers and Fordham University students. They followed a group of Fordham kids into the Arthur Avenue Retail Market building to see where they were going.

Through the group of glass double doors, A.J. and Logan passed an open, cigar rolling area on the left and an open pastry and coffee store on the right. *This place doesn't look or smell as good as De Lillo's,* A.J. thought.

Nice...that redhead with the Ram's jacket is very cute. And she smiled at me when she held the door open, Logan fantasized.

There was a butcher on the right, and in the distance, the Jersey kids spotted a line of people standing in line at an Italian delicatessen. They would soon find out that this is the Mecca of delis in the entire city of New York. But that would be much later. On the left side of the market, before a few rows of long tables was what attracted the Fordham students. A bar. It's a full service bar, with every one of the twelve stools occupied, and a row of young people standing behind them, all drinking beer.

The red head and her two, cute brunette friends took notice of Logan's maroon, Ridgewood Crew Jacket.

"Hey, Ridgewood! I'm from Fair Lawn, we are practically neighbors," Colleen Dunn said.

"We're from Connecticut, so we have no idea where Ridgewood is," one of the other girls said, laughing.

"Jersey...it's near me in Jersey!" Colleen laughed.

"I'm Logan, this is A.J."

"Are you both at Fordham, or just looking at schools?" Coleen asked.

"Actually, I'm going to Columbia in the fall and A.J. is...."

"Brown University," A.J. finished Logan's thought.

"Excuse us, we have the Ivy League amongst us. This calls for a beer," Colleen quipped.

"Ahh, we can't. We aren't twenty one," A.J. said.

"Neither are we. The bartender is my sister. What do you want?" Colleen said.

"I guess a beer," Logan said.

This is my first, illegal beer served at a bar. I'm gonna go for it, A.J. said to herself.

"A Corona, with a lime," A.J. blurted.

"Smart and sophisticated as well," One of the girls said laughingly.

"Are you guys a couple?" Colleen asked. She directed her question to A.J. but glanced at Logan.

"Oh no, we are doing a semester in the Bronx as a social experiment," A.J. responded.

As A.J. began to explain the Spechler Program, Colleen handed everyone beers. They all clinked bottles in a toast. Colleen maneuvered so she could speak to Logan while A.J. explained the program to her unusually, attentive friends.

"Too bad you're not coming to Fordham in the fall. It's a great school and a lot of fun," Colleen said.

"I can see that. I might gain fifty pounds living around this place. The food is awesome," Logan replied.

"It sure makes up for the crap they feed us in the cafeteria at Fordham. It's toxic," Colleen laughed.

The banter went back and forth for a good while. Four beers worth. A.J. was feeling woozy. Logan felt he should stop with the beer. Logan realized he was starving for something to eat. The three, Fordham students had to go back to the campus and invited A.J. and Logan.

The Ridgewood kids declined the invite and headed for Mike's Deli for sandwiches, but not before Colleen and Logan exchanged cell numbers, and one of the two brunettes squeezed her cell number into A.J..'s hand.

❈

Logan and A.J. took a Gypsy cab to The Hub. It was only about twenty-five blocks from where they were, but it was getting cold quickly. The twelve-minute ride was well worth the eight-dollar fare.

"What do you think we will do tonight?" A.J. asked

"Loida and her friends said they will meet us on the corner of Third and 149th. They know a good place. Some sort of hip hop concert I think," Logan responded.

"Should be fun. I read somewhere hip hop started in the South Bronx. I'd rather see a Taylor Swift concert, but...

"But she would never dream of doing a concert in this neighborhood?" Logan finished A.J.'s thought.

"What about Yankee Stadium? That's not too far from here, Logan."

"Maybe J-LO, but Taylor Swift? I'm not so sure," Logan said.
"Anyway, where are we meeting them again?"

CHAPTER 15

07050

The first time Rosa and Semaj saw Mr. Taylor in the daylight since they moved in, was on that Saturday. Mr. Taylor was home every night for dinner and the table discussions were lively and interesting. He was truly interested in their lives in the Bronx and their schooling.

After a quick cup of coffee, while his boarders were having breakfast, Mr. Taylor was off to his country club for breakfast with his friends and then on to an indoor driving range in Paramus for a lesson to work on his "pathetic, golf swing."

Mrs. Taylor was off at the gym working on her "huge butt." Her rear was anything but that. *She could be a model for J. Crew*, Rosa thought. Semaj pretended not to hear, but he couldn't help notice how attractive of a mom she was.

"I just can't relate to this lifestyle," Rosa said. After the house was empty, she and Semaj were getting ready to be picked up by their new classmates and friends.

"Naturally, these are the one percent we hear all about. I'm just happy to be exposed to this life," Semaj said.

"As if we are ever going to get there!" Rosa said.

"Do I have to give you another pep talk, Rosa? This is America; we can do whatever we want with our lives. What if you become a well-known doctor and make a bunch of money? Will you stay on Fox Street and hear sirens and shots fired every other night?"

"I can tell you where I won't live. It's here. I intend to use my education and language to help other Hispanics and your people. I will work for an emergency room at a city hospital. Money isn't everything in life," Rosa declared.

"Very noble of you. Me? I'm going for the gusto in life. I want to be rich. There is a better way to live and that life awaits me. With education, luck, hard work, and faith in my Lord and Savior, I can do anything."

"I wish you all the best. It's just not my thing. Not that living this way is bad. It has a price!" Rosa said.

"Okay, shoot!"

"Some of these kids are a mess. You can cut their anxiety with a knife. A few of the girls I met have been cutters, some with eating disorders. Maybe I should have had anorexia for a while to lose some weight," Rosa laughed.

"Stop being so hard on yourself."

"No really. There are a lot of kids seeing shrinks and taking anxiety meds here. The pressure on them is amazing. Anyone I know at Clinton who is seeing a shrink it's because it's court ordered," Rosa said.

"I hear that. But what if you added intense academic pressure to the lives we lead in the hood. What kind of..."

"I have no idea. That could be a monster which can rule the world," Rosa contemplated.

"Let's see how we come out after a semester here. Maybe we can make a difference to the world."

A car horn beeped and Semaj ran to the front door. "It's for you. My ride is coming soon. Where are you guys off to?"

"To West Point for a hockey game. Steph's brother is a cadet there. He is a forward on the Army hockey team. It's like less than an hour away."

"Another great experience in the life of a future, legal aid attorney. Have fun," Semaj quipped.

Rosa put her parka on and headed for the door.

"What are you doing today?"

"You know Nicole Radcliff? She's picking me up and we're going to the mall for lunch and a movie, her treat," Semaj smiled.

"Ooh, your first date with a rich, white chick. How nice."

"Life is wonderful!" Semaj declared. Rosa made a crinkly face of disdain and left to see Army play Air Force in a BMW 340i.

CHAPTER 16

HEATING UP

At eight that Saturday evening A.J. and Logan waited at the center of the Hub for about ten minutes before Loida Milan showed up with a few of her girlfriends.

Two, white kids, waiting on 149th Street and Third Avenue was not a common sight. A.J. was bundled up in a down parka, Logan in his Ridgewood Crew jacket. They lingered on Arthur Avenue for a while, sobering up from the afternoon beers they had with Colleen and company. A stuffed, Mike's deli sandwich, a few cups of espresso at De Lillo's, and a couple of slices of Full Moon pizza did the trick.

"Hey guys, so glad you could come. I thought maybe you would have stood us up," Loida said. A comely wink to Logan said volumes.

It never crossed my mind, you horny bitch, A.J. thought.

"No way. This is our first, real, hip-hop concert," Logan said.

"It's not really a concert but there are a few artists who will perform, and some Latin dancing too. We can teach you how to dance a little salsa," Loida declared as she gyrated her hips. Her friends joined in for the impromptu ten-second-dance recital. Obviously, more for Logan's attention than for A.J.'s.

"Where are we going?" A.J. asked.

"A place called The Point. It's the only place people our age can go to where there is no trouble, no booze, and great music. And the best thing is there is no cover charge," Loida explained.

Amazing, she has her head on straight after all, A.J. thought.

"Look it...none of us needs no trouble. It's time we grew up anyways," one of her posse said in a thick, Bronx-Spanglish accent.

The group started walking. In a few minutes they arrived at The Point. A.J. and Logan were both surprised at what they saw. A large and colorful graffiti mural on an adjacent wall announced they had arrived. The Point is a storefront community center which is largely dedicated to youth development and the cultural and economic revitalization of the Hunt's Point section of the South Bronx.

Two, large Hispanic security guards signed each visitor in, checking the bags of each girl. A.J. received a big hello and welcome from both men. She was as rare as a black pearl. They eyed Logan with a warning look which told him to keep in line or be thrown out on his ear. A pass of a metal detector wand on everyone made certain nothing bad was being concealed. The handbags of all the girls were inspected.

"Hey A.J.," a familiar voice called out. It was Keith Copeland who was already inside the point.

"Keith! You made it!" A.J. said.

"I wouldn't be any where else tonight. You are in for a treat," Keith said. His warm smile also spoke volumes. Keith hugged A.J. and then gave Logan the half-shoulder hug.

My mom should see me now. She would faint dead away, Logan thought.

The main room was already crowded. Remy Wap's song *Fetty Wap* blared on The Point's speaker system. The white-tiled floors of the room could hardly be seen because of the large crowd moving to the music.

"Yo, this song is in your honor. Fetty is from Paterson, New Jersey," Keith announced.

"Yeah, we know. He's amazing!" A.J. said.

He sucks! Logan thought.

As the night continued the music of Jay Z, *Picasso Baby*, and a few, Fat Joe songs, like *Terror Squad* and 50 Cent, *We Taken Over*, banged on the eardrums of the dancers.

Jesus Christ, Almighty, Logan thought. That was his dad's favorite saying when he heard hip-hop.

"Now this is real, Bronx hip-hop," Keith declared as Fat Joe's music banged on.

Keith danced along with A.J. for most of the hip-hop tunes.

Loida begged the DJ to play some Latin music. The DJ finally succumbed to her pleas. She immediately pulled Logan aside and tried to teach him her moves. Logan looked like a scared rabbit, moving his feet like a white boy from Ridgewood.

Keith took the opportunity to take a break and he and A.J. grabbed their coats and stepped outside onto the cold, gray concrete pavement.

"So how do you like the hood, so far?" Keith asked.

"It's different. Very different," A.J. replied.

"Is that a good or bad different?"

"I wouldn't classify it either way. Just very different than I've ever seen," A.J. said.

"I guess so. Just for your information, the population of this area is two-thirds Hispanic and a third African-American. Over forty-percent of the people are below the federal poverty level. That in itself is a lot different than you are used to, I would imagine," Keith said, looking into A.J.'s eyes for her response.

"I'm learning something new every day I'm here," A.J. replied.

A group of young Hispanic men were passing by in a shiny, black BMW. The guy in the passenger seat rolled down the car's window and shouted out to A.J.

"Mira, mommie. What's up?"

ZIP CODE

This was the best catcall he could conjure up at the moment? Keith thought.

"*Coño*," Keith said in a low voice.

"What's that mean?" A.J. said.

"Oh nothing. Just a really bad, Spanish word! He certainly has good taste in women, though."

"Thank you, Keith. That was nice of you to say," A.J. offered.

"From the first time I saw you I knew you were a real beauty and a real lady," Keith said. He got closer to A.J., leaned down and kissed her on her lips.

It wasn't the first time A.J. was ever kissed, but it was the first time a black kid was ever that close.

"Let's go inside. I'm really cold," A.J. said. She liked the kiss, but didn't want to lead Keith on.

Inside The Point, in the corner of the room, Logan and Loida were in a full make out session.

ZIP CODE

CHAPTER 17

07030

Hoboken, New Jersey.

Nicole took Semaj to Hoboken to walk around trendy Washington Avenue where seemingly thousands of yupsters use two weeks of their pay for rent. Many of these young college graduates have at least one roommate, with some having up to five friends to help pay for the enormously priced leases.

It took Nicole thirty minutes, driving around the streets to find a parking spot. Finally, she pulled into a garage.

"I should have just pulled in here to begin with," Nicole commented.

"It must be expensive to park here," Semaj added.

"Who cares, it's my dad's credit card. He never questions what I buy."

"Do you get an allowance?"

"Ahh…No! I just get what I want. Dad is good like that," Nicole quipped.

"Dude, I wish I had a dad like that. I never even knew my father. Mom had me when she was seventeen and it's been her and me ever since," Semaj said in a matter-of-fact tone.

"So this is yupster central. I'm not even sure what a yupster is," Nicole admitted.

They stopped into a Starbucks to get out of the chilled air and have a hot *cappuccino*.

"If you really want to know, I can tell you about all this country's generations from the early nineteen-hundreds. I did a sociology report on that. That report and my grades are actually what got me to come to Ridgewood," Semaj said.

"Way cool! Sure, tell me about it," Nicole said. She had an incredible memory and was an eager leaner. Her four point zero average came easy. Nicole is destined for the Ivy League and med school. Nicole has it all. Brains, great looks with long, black hair, big, sky-blue eyes, and a body which is the envy of most girls at Ridgewood. Nicole is the absolute fantasy of every boy in the school.

"Okay, stop me if I bore you. First, there was The Lost Generation. They were born in the late, eighteen hundreds until nineteen hundred. They fought in World War One. Hemingway named The Lost Generation and wrote a few books about them. His books are still relevant and amazing. Then came The Greatest Generation. They were born in the early nineteen hundreds. They grew up during the great depression and fought in World War Two. They fought for what was right and really worked together to fight the Nazis and the Japanese. Bored yet?" Semaj asked.

"Not at all, go on," Nicole replied. Semaj, and his knowledge of American history fascinated the Ridgewood High heartthrob. She had become mesmerized at how handsome Semaj was.

ZIP CODE

"Cool! Interesting tid-bit. Newsman Tom Brokaw named The Greatest Generation. He wrote a best-selling book on the subject. After them came The Silent Generation. They were born during the great depression and expected life to suck. For most of them, it was true. Then came the baby boomers. They were children of The Greatest Generation. That is my favorite group. Nineteen forty-five through nineteen sixty-four. They lived in the most prosperous time in our history. They went through the Cold War with Russia, worried about nuclear attack, saw Kennedy assassinated, saw the first man walk on the moon, and that silly war in Vietnam. I almost forgot... and the civil rights movement.

"Still interested?" Semaj checked.

"Amazing, yes! Your eyes sparkle when you talk about this."

"Thanks, I love the subject. Okay, now came Generation X. They had a lower birthrate than their parents. Big on education. They saw fighting in the first Gulf War, and the decline of communist Russia. Along came The Millennials. The Internet, huge economic decline in two thousand and eight. Nearly as bad as the great depression. The terrorist attacks on the World Trade Center, Facebook, global warming, and the invasion of Iraq. And now us... Generation Z. Cell phones, iPods, and the digital world. Information at our fingertips and a sucky economy. And that's my report. Thank you, ladies and gentleman," Semaj laughed.

Nicole was enthralled. "You are so amazing, Semaj. And very cute if you don't mind my saying so."

Semaj felt his face blush, but his dark complexion didn't reveal a hue.

"Thanks Nicole, I'm not used to being complimented," Semaj admitted.

"Let's head back. We can go to my house and listen to some music and hang out. My parents are at a wedding in Maryland. Some cousin on my mom's side. Real Daughters of the American Revolution types."

※

Rosa was having a great time. That is, until one of the girls started talking about her diet.

"Army kicked Air Force's ass today. I'm so happy for my brother, Dan. And he scored his twelfth goal!" Steph announced.

"He is so hot, Stephanie. I've had a crush on him since seventh grade," Michelle Giordano said. She was one of the girls who made the trip to West Point.

"Get on a long line, Mich. This guy gets more girls than Leo DiCaprio. I can't even!" Steph said.

"Well, put in a good word for me, will you?" Michelle said.

All of the girls laughed as they lined up to get some lunch at a snack stand.

"I can't eat this crap. Let's get on the road and stop somewhere for a salad," Michelle said.

"A hot dog is fine for me," Steph said.

ZIP CODE

"Me too. And they smell so great!" Rosa said.

"Rosa, if you ever want to lose weight, that's not what you should be eating," Michelle said.

Rosa felt like she was punched in the stomach. *Fuck you too,* Rosa thought.

"Mich, that is so rude!" Steph said.

"Just sayin'. Sorry, Rosa, if I offended you," Michelle said.

"No worries," Rosa replied. She felt the tears welling in her eyes.

✤

Nicole and Semaj were back in Ridgewood at her home. It was as big and luxurious as the Taylors' place. Nicole's dad is a well-known, orthopedic surgeon and her mom is a psychiatrist. Their home, "Tall Pines" made Semaj's mouth fall open like Jay Z's.

Nicole went into the kitchen and came back with two Heinekens. Down to the family room they went. The room was like something out of a magazine. Yankee memorabilia, bats, balls, game-worn jerseys and a slew of autographed photos to Doc Radcliffe from Derek Jeter to C.C. Sabathia, and other Yankee greats from current players to back in the day. A huge, pool table, a full, Yankee-themed bar, an antique jukebox, and an amazing eighty-inch, flat screen television with a surround system second to none. Semaj was blown away.

"Let's put on some music and chill, okay?" Nicole asked.

"Sure, what a place to chill!" Semaj blurted. He thought he had died and gone to heaven.

Nicole put a Taylor Swift CD on and was not shy with the volume. She made two more trips to the kitchen for more Heinekens. "I've asked my dad to stock these down here, but he only has room for three kinds of beer on tap," Nicole lamented.

"Whatever, this is good." Semaj said.

"Let's dance!"

Nicole popped in an Adele CD and found one of her favorites, *Chasing Pavements*.

Semaj and Nicole danced close together, she still holding her beer behind her dance partner's neck. She offered a kiss and Semaj willingly took it.

Hours passed and the two kids from polar different worlds became more than just friends.

CHAPTER 18

TROUBLE AT 10468

A.J. and Logan had the trip to DeWitt Clinton down pat. After the first week at school, the train ride from the South Bronx was all but routine. They had their bagel and coffee each morning while riding on the train as Sonia never woke in time to prepare breakfast. A.J. was now expert at ignoring any of the furtive glances from creepy, older men, or remarks from any students from Clinton or the other schools in the area.

Logan mostly listened to music on his ear buds. Sometimes the gentle rocking of the train would put him into a semi-conscious snooze.

The second Monday morning at Clinton started off the same as the prior week, except this day was windy and much colder. The smell and feel of snow was in the air.

When Logan and A.J. descended the stairs at the Jerome Avenue station, A.J. saw two of her classmates along with Keith, and walked to the school together with them. Logan was in his own world, and hustled to get out of the cold, morning air.

As he approached the place where the first day of school's stabbing occurred, three, Hispanic boys approached Logan. Three guys who he didn't recognize as students.

"Yo, tough guy, waz up?" one said. The other two fanned out, placing Logan in the middle of them.

Now what? Logan thought.

"Sorry, do I know you?" Logan said.

"You don't know me, but you know my sister."

"Your sister?"

"Yeah, nigga, my sister, Loida? You were seen with her on Saturday night." His name was Ephraim Milan. A tough looking, short, dark Puerto Rican, with a flame tattoo which jutted out of his jacket collar up his neck, ending just under his angular chin. His jet-black hair was slicked back with lots of hair product.

"Yeah, we hung out at The Point," Logan admitted.

"I'm told you and her were all over each other. You a handsy guy," Ephraim said.

"Look, dude, I don't want any trouble," Logan said. Heeding Sonia's advice, Logan tried to walk past the fiery-eyed Ephraim. Loida's enraged brother stood in his way.

"Nigga, you think you gonna come here, do what you want with our women, and go back and tell you *maricon* friends all Spanish girls is easy? Tell them they all *putas*?" Ephraim challenged.

"Nothing happened, dude. Loida is a nice girl, and we're just friends," Logan said. He remembered the string of texts sent to his friends, telling them about his steamy evening at The Point.

ZIP CODE

"You wanna tell her boyfriend when he gets off Rikers next month, you *hijo de puta?* Or maybe I tell him instead," Efraim said, moving closer to the now scared Logan.

Okay, I get it. Stay away from Loida. I hear you," Logan said.

"It ain't that easy, pappi. Maybe we kick your white ass right here so you understand our ways, my Jersey nigga.

A loud and familiar voice rang out from the steps of Clinton.

"Back away, now!" Mr. Taveleres shouted. He and two security guards ran toward the group.

"This ain't over, *pendejo.*" Ephraim said. He and his two sidekicks slowly walked away, leaving the shaken Logan standing at the spot where they accosted him.

"What was that about, Logan?" Mr. Taveleres asked.

One of the two security guards spoke into his two-way, telling whoever was listening to stand down.

"I...I...went out with that guy's sister, Loida Milan, on Saturday night. Nothing really happened, Mr. Taveleres."

"To him something happened. Come on, lets go inside."

Taveleres put his arm around Logan, and they walked into the principal's office.

"Logan, as I'm sure you already know, this is a far different world than you live in. It's a macho thing. This guy is protecting his sister. She is like his property. I suggest you stay clear of her. I don't want to see you as a casualty of this punk. I need to report this to Mr. Spechler. This could end your stay here at Clinton, I'm afraid," Mr. Taveleres said.

"I'm sure there is a way we can handle this, sir. I'm not one to run away from a problem. I'm telling you all we did was make out a little," Logan argued.

"To that maniac, it's as if you went all the way. Maybe we can speak with Loida and see if she can calm the situation down. Until then, I have to report this and also tell your sponsor, Sergeant Colon. I can't allow you to ride the trains right now, buddy."

"I understand. You need to do what you think is best. I'm truly sorry for this, Mr. Taveleres."

"Okay, go about your day. I'll alert security inside to be extra vigilant until we get to the bottom of this."

07450

Meanwhile, back in Ridgewood...

ZIP CODE

Rosa was still disturbed about the insensitive remark from Michelle at West Point. She didn't bring it up to Semaj on Sunday. Semaj was picked up again by Nicole and was gone for most of the day. When he was home that evening, he seemed engrossed with texting on his cell phone. Rosa told Steph she needed to chill and study. She demurred on an invite to go ice-skating.

At breakfast the next morning, Rosa decided to speak with Mrs. Taylor.

"Good morning, Rosa, you seemed quiet yesterday. Everything okay?" Mrs. Taylor asked. She already knew what Rosa's problem was. Steph told her mom about the unfortunate remark and Steph's mom had called Mrs. Taylor to tell her what had occurred.

"I have a question if you don't mind," Rosa said.

"Sure, anything."

"You said you were a nutritionist. I think I may need your help."

"You want to learn how to eat right and lose weight, I suppose," Mrs. Taylor said.

"Yes, something like that. I've been a bit chunky my whole life, and I think it's time I take care of myself a bit better." Rosa felt the tears coming back into her eyes.

"What brought this on, sweetheart?"

"Just an off handed remark that hurt...it really hurt," Rosa admitted. The tears began to flow down her cheeks.

"I'm sorry about that, but I heard you say something very important. You said you wanted to take care of yourself. Not that you need to lose weight for anyone but yourself. For your health and well being. Well, Rosa you came to the right person, and I'm enormously flattered."

"Thank you so much, Mrs. Taylor. Can you help?" Rosa asked, dabbing away her tears.

"I can and I will. Here's what we are going to do...together. It's pretty simple. Proper nutrition, and I will make a comprehensive plan for you. Along with the right kind of exercise. We will start today, right now! I will get you with a personal trainer starting tomorrow. We will work around your school schedule."

"I really can't afford that, Mrs. Taylor."

"Who said anything about you paying for this? Mr. Taylor and I would be delighted to help you. And this is just between us, Rosa." Mrs. Taylor hugged Rosa as a mother would.

"Now let's pick some good, breakfast choices." Mrs. Taylor said.

CHAPTER 19

Ghetto Lessons

A.J. and Logan were asked to report to Mr. Taveleres' office at the end of the school day. When they arrived, Sonia was there to collect them and bring them back to her Fox Street apartment. The three of them met with the principal and discussed the events at The Point on Saturday night, reviewed their options, and left the school.

It was the first time the Jersey kids were ever in a patrol car. They stared at the car's dashboard like little kids at show and tell.

Sonia broke the ice and revisited the events of Saturday night past.

"Okay, lets go over it one more time. You were both at The Point listening to music and dancing. Logan, you and this Loida chick were dancing and then making out in the corner. Some touchy, feely...and that was it. And A.J. you were hanging out with Keith until the Latin music came on, then you went outside for a few minutes. You came back in because it was cold and danced and hung out some more. Anything else?" Sonia asked.

"That's about it," Logan replied.

"Sure, that's it." A.J. said.

"A.J. did you see Logan and Miss Loida in the corner?"

"Nope. The place was pretty crowded."

"What time did you leave, how did you get home, and what time did you arrive back at the apartment?" Sonia asked. She wanted to get the story and timeline straight.

"We left about one. Took a Gypsy home and got back in five or ten minutes," Logan stated.

"Okay. When we get home I need to make a few calls. My Captain knows about the story and he told me I could do what needed to be done. I have no idea what to do here, but I know someone who does."

Sonia called a dear friend who was her mentor at NYPD. Vic Cipullo, A First Grade Detective and Vice President of the Detectives' Endowment Association. Vic is a forty-two year, NYPD veteran, and very near retirement. He was one of the top ten Super Cops back in his early career. Vic was well connected from the commissioner's office to the street-crossing guards. If anyone could, Vic would know the direction they should go to put this fire out.

Vic picked up his phone on one ring.

"Hi, babydoll. How ya doin'?" Vic asked.

"Mostly good, with the exception of a brand new headache I have," Sonia said.

"Talk to me!"

ZIP CODE

"The Jersey student who's staying with me was accosted by an asswipe and two of his goons for going out with his sister on one date this past Saturday. Vic, Logan is a good boy. A real, nice kid," Sonia explained.

"He's family as far as I'm concerned, Sonia. Tell me more," Vic said.

"The mutt's name is Efraim Milan. His sister is Loida Milan. She is a student at Clinton. I think she's a junior there. Anyway, the principal said she's been no problem at all. Logan made out with her, that's all. This knucklehead shows up at the school today ready to rumble."

"Nothing nasty? I mean with Logan and the sister?" Vic asked.

"No. Just swapped spit," Sonia replied.

"Give me an hour. Stay put; keep the kid close. I've seen bad stuff happen over sisters." Vic hung up.

Fifteen minutes later, Cipullo called back.

"Babydoll, I have what we need. Now, listen up. This Efraim dude is bad news. Long rap sheet...robbery, distribution, some strong arm, and street stuff. He did three years inside. All at the ripe age of twenty-two. My guy over in the four-one tells me his family is good people. The sister is tied up with a real gang-banger scumbag by the name of Pedro Ponce, AKA P.P. My guy thinks the girl may have had a kid with him. The baby daddy is inside on a two year stint and will be paroled soon. We can stall the parole, but I don't think that's the way to go. I also know this Efraim's parole officer. She and I were an item once. Still good friends. We can violate Efraim on a terrorist threat and he goes back inside, but I don't like that at all either. Best thing to do is me and my guy in the four-one sit down with our boy Efraim and reason with him. We give him some favor he may need down the road and tell him the kid is off limits. I'm sure we can resolve this nicely. Now, tell me, are you still seeing that loser lieutenant from the five-two?" Vic asked.

"I can't talk about that right now," Sonia replied.

"For the tenth time, he's no good for you. Dump his sorry butt," Vic scolded Sonia.

"I hear you, Godfather. What do I do with these kids right now?"

"I'm on it. I'll call you when the coast is clear. It's all gonna be fine. I'll call you tonight or early morning. Kisses," Vic said and hung up.

Sonia turned to the nervously awaiting Logan and A.J. She wasn't angry with Logan, just angry at the situation he accidentally found himself in.

"Logan, honey. You did nothing wrong. Nothing any red-blooded, American man wouldn't do. It's just that down here, women can be dangerous. They can be more dangerous than a nine-millimeter or a long knife. My friend, Vic thinks he can settle this. Tonight, we take in a nice pizza and watch television. Tomorrow, I take you both to school," Sonia said.

"Thanks, Sonia. I have to tell you something. Loida keeps calling my cell and texting. She wants to talk. She feels real bad about her brother. And Mr. Spechler has called twice," Logan said.

ZIP CODE

"Okay, just text her back and tell her you need time to sort this out with me. You can't afford to piss her off. And call Mr. Spechler. I'll speak with him if he wants. It's all going to be fine.

Logan leaned back in the kitchen chair and exhaled a sigh of relief.

A.J. ran to the bathroom to be sick. She didn't think about the cockroaches.

CHAPTER 20

Rosa got to her homeroom class a bit early on Monday morning, after her talk with Mrs. Taylor. She found Michelle Giordano waiting for her.

"I hope you don't hate me, Rosa," Michelle said. She seemed sincere and contrite, but Rosa was on her guard.

"Hate you? Why would I hate you, Mich?" Rosa replied. Rosa wanted to make sure this spoiled, rich girl wasn't playing her.

"That remark I made about your weight was uncalled for, and I really apologize."

"It really did hurt. Hey, you know what? It finally got me off my butt, and I'm going to do something about it now. I just hope I can follow through," Rosa said.

"The words just came out of my big mouth and I knew it was dumb the minute I said what I said. Listen, I'm Italian! We eat like crazy at my house, and I was chubby growing up. I had an eating disorder in like the fifth grade because everyone in my family was overweight and I had self-esteem issues. I could have died from what I was doing. I should have known better than to talk like that to you." Michelle had tears in her eyes. She turned her head not to let the other kids see as they began to enter the classroom.

Rosa sensed Michelle was being genuine.

"That's what friends are for, Mich. Let's put this behind us. I have a lot more to be concerned about than extra pounds. I'm finding the workload here to be a lot more challenging than Clinton. I don't want to leave here thinking I couldn't hack the work," Rosa confessed.

"Can I do anything to help? How about we do a study group? I mean it!"

"That may really help me. Honestly, I don't want anyone to think the ghetto chick is not good enough," Rosa admitted.

"I don't see you as some ghetto chick. Some others may, but our group of friends are all pulling for you. It must be real hard for you seeing all this wealth and stuff, knowing you have to go back...there I go again saying the wrong thing again. What an ass!" Michelle said.

"I get it, and you're right. I would love to know how A.J. and Logan are doing in the hood. Until you have lived in both worlds, you have no idea how different things are thirty minutes away."

"I've heard some rumors. Logan and A.J. are having a tough time of it. You know, adapting to the environment."

"Why? Did anything happen?" Rosa asked.

"I just heard Logan's parents want to bring him back home. There was some issue, but I have no specifics."

"I'll text my friends at Clinton and find out. In the meantime, let's talk more about that study group after school." Rosa was encouraged.

ZIP CODE

By lunchtime, Rosa got the scoop on Loida Milan and Logan, and the altercation outside of Clinton. Also in the rumor mill at Ridgewood was the budding romance between Semaj and Nicole. Nicole told two of her friends about her hookup with Semaj, and the word was traveling throughout the senior class.

Rosa heard the news and texted Semaj:

> Dude, we need to talk!
>
> Sure, I'm skipping lunch and going to the library
>
> After school!

❦

Logan spoke by phone with Mr. Spechler on Sunday night. Spechler was going to the Bronx to meet with Logan, Mr. Taveleres, and Sonia Colon after school on Monday. Logan's parents wanted Mr. Spechler to pull the plug on the program.

They would make a decision after they all met.

CHAPTER 21

BIG SIT DOWN IN THE HOOD

Detective Vic Cipullo and his friend in the four-one precinct, Steve Centeneo, met with Efraim Milan at Fort Apache. The nickname was given to the four-one back in the day when the Bronx was literally burning down.

"Efraim, thanks for coming in." Centeneo began the meeting.

"Yo, either I came in or you came and got me. Waz up?" Efraim asked.

"I'm Detective Cipullo from NYPD Intelligence. We heard about the problem at Clinton. You and that Jersey kid," Vic said.

"Do I have to lawyer up?" Efraim asked.

"Look, it's just three guys talkin'. We don't have any charges against you, and we don't plan any at this point. I can violate your probation, but that's not on the table just yet," Centeneo added.

"What's your problem with this kid?" Vic asked.

"He took advantage of my sister. I can't have that. I have a reputation, dude."

"Just a little kissing is not taking advantage of your sister Efraim. She's a big girl," Centeneo said.

"I heard it was a lot more than that. My guy tells me they went out the back door of The Point. That Jersey *maricon* needs to know that ain't right. Just because he rich, an' shit." Efraim was flashing his dark, angry eyes.

" That's not the information we have, but regardless, your sister is of age and she has the right to make her own decisions without you stepping in. This has to end here and now and I want your word," Vic said.

"Or what?" Efraim blurted.

"There you go, getting all pissed off again. We're not here to threaten you, Efraim. We know as good as you how the street works. You are going to need us down the road. Detective Centeneo and me have a way of looking away at certain things. You can use friends in the NYPD right?" Vic reasoned.

"I'm listening!" Efraim stated.

"We know your crew is hustling girls on Southern Boulevard. We also know you have a business selling some dope in the Hub. I can come down really hard on your operation or we can...let's just say we can not come down so hard," Centeneo said.

"This kid is like family to me, son. Let your sister work out her relationships. Leave Logan Darby alone, and we stay cool with you," Vic offered.

"And when P.P. finds out? What then?" Efraim said.

ZIP CODE

"We ain't gonna tell him, and neither should you," Centeneo said.

"P.P.'s a scumbag anyway. He never support my sister and her kid anyway," Efraim added.

"So we have a deal? I need your word, buddy," Vic said.

"It's all good. You got my word," Efraim stated.

Efraim left Fort Apache, and Vic immediately called Sonia.

"Babydoll, it's all done. The coast is clear for your boy," Vic said.

"My, Godfather! You are the best. You never let me down," Sonia said. She was relieved.

"One thing, though. The knucklehead said there was more to it. He heard your Jersey kid and his sister took a quick trip outside of The Point. Could be bullshit, but who knows? Tell Logan to keep his cool with the hood girls, okay?"

"I'll get that message to him five-by-five," Sonia said in cop talk which meant loud and clear.

※

Mr. Spechler, as promised, met with Mr. Taveleres, Logan, and Sonia in the principal's office after the school day had ended.

"Logan, your parents are apoplectic over what happened yesterday. They want to end your part of the program, which means A.J. has to go home as well."

"May I say something here?" Sonia asked.

"Absolutely, Sergeant," Mr. Taveleres said.

"The heat is off with Efraim Milan. He met with two detectives and agreed to stand down. They reasoned with Loida's brother, and he will back off. I believe there will be no more repercussions," Sonia said. She flashed an icy stare at Logan. He knew by her look he would be hearing more from her on the matter.

"This experiment is very important in the academic community. It can work as a bridge toward understanding and lessening hate and prejudice. Not just here, but throughout the whole country. We can do something really meaningful, or we can close up shop and say there is no hope. Logan, you need to show more discretion and behave like a gentleman. Do you want to stay?" Mr. Spechler asked.

"I do. I absolutely do. I can see some great things happening here, and I want to be part of a solution. For me to quit now… for me to leave just adds to the rich kid reputation. If I give up now, it shows I can avoid any conflict or problem as I grow up. I'm not a quitter, Mr. Spechler."

"I know you're not. You are one of the best students who ever walked the halls at Ridgewood, and your future is very bright. I'm happy you feel the way you do. It shows great determination and maturity. Now I have to go back and convince your parents," Mr. Spechler said.

ZIP CODE

After some more discussion, the meeting ended. Mr. Spechler went back to Ridgewood, Mr. Taveleres saw to his after-school programs, and Sonia took Logan back to Fox Street. They got into Sonia's personal car. A.J. sat in the front. Logan in the rear.

Sonia adjusted her rear view mirror. Her big, brown eyes, full of anger, caught Logan's attention.

"You freakin' lied to me, Logan. You flat out lied!" Sonia hollered.

"Lied? When did I lie?" Logan asked.

"We heard you and little Miss Loida, the unwed mother of an eighteen month old, didn't stay inside The Point all night. What do you have to say for yourself?" Sonia was furious.

"Well...well," Logan stammered.

"So it's true, then. Did you know anything about this, A.J.? Sonia asked.

"I swear to God. No, I didn't," A.J. replied. She turned and looked at Logan. He was looking down at his hands.

"Look it, mister studly, mister *que cojones*. Never lie to me again. And watch your ass around here. Got it?" Sonia sounded like she came from the hood. Indeed she did.

"I'm truly sorry, Sonia. I apologize. Nothing like this will happen again," Logan said.

LOUIS ROMANO

CHAPTER 22

Mr. Spechler met with the Taylors and the Darbys the evening he returned from his meeting at DeWitt Clinton. They all met at Ridgewood High. A.J. and Logan's parents were quite anxious to hear the results of Mr. Spechler's conference. They met in the main office of the school.

"Thank you all for coming. I met with A.J., Logan, Clinton's Principal, and Sergeant Sonia Colon. First, I have to tell you the kids are doing fine. They are adjusting to the environment and participating tremendously in the program. It's a tremendous learning experience for both of them. You should be very proud of these great students," Mr. Spechler began.

"With all due respect, I was proud of Logan way before this program of yours. I think it's time he comes home and finishes his senior year in Ridgewood," Kyle Darby said.

"I, for one, am very worried for his safety...and for A.J.'s as well," Kathy Darby added.

Mr. Spechler took some notes and paused before answering the parents.

"And how do you feel about the situation Mr. and Mrs. Taylor?" Spechler asked.

"I agree with the Darbys at this point. Whatever happened with that Spanish girl and Logan seems to have put both kids in harm's way," Lilly Taylor said.

"First of all, she's not Spanish. She's a Puerto Rican. They are very different than Spanish people. They are the scourge of the Caribbean in my book," Kyle interrupted.

Arthur Taylor looked at Kyle Darby and cleared his throat.

"I'm really here with an open mind to hear what you discovered, Mr. Spechler, and then we can make an intelligent decision about going forward with the program," Arthur Taylor said.

"From what I was able to ascertain, yes, there was a problem and Logan was approached by the girl's brother. Mr. Taveleres personally handled the situation with extreme diligence and made sure both Logan and A.J. were safe," Mr. Spechler said.

"What did he do, give them bullet proof vests? These animals have nothing to lose," Kyle Darby interrupted again.

"Please allow me to finish, Mr. Darby. Sonia Colon is a New York City Police Sergeant, as you all know. She was immediately contacted by Mr. Taveleres and secured both A.J. and Logan. Ms. Colon wisely contacted a colleague who is in NYPD intelligence, who together with a detective from the local precinct, spoke with the brother who had approached Logan," Mr. Spechler continued.

"You mean the brother who accosted my son, Mr. Spechler, not approached him," Kathy Darby said.

"Fine, I will use the word accosted if it fits better for you. The important thing to understand here is the police were successful in defusing the situation. They are convinced no further problems will occur. Logan will not be accosted again by the brother or his friends," Mr. Spechler said.

"And you believe that, Spechler? You honestly believe these savages will forgive and forget whatever happened between my son and this slut? I, for one, do not trust in the word of criminals," Kyle said.

"Mr. Darby, you are painting a very, bad portrait of these people, and you are refusing to believe in the word of professionals who know the culture far better than we do," Spechler added.

"I would like to hear what Logan and A.J. think. They are not dumb kids who will continue in this program if they are afraid for their own safety. They entered this program with the full understanding the Bronx is not Disney World. They are both trying to achieve something which can actually make a difference in this world. Please tell us where A.J.'s and Logan's heads are at. "Do they want to continue or not?" Arthur Taylor offered.

"That is a very good question. I spoke at some length with your children. They both feel, and this is them speaking, not me, that leaving now will be a great defeat for them. Logan especially wants to prove to himself that running and quitting on the program, because of a bump in the road is not in his long-term, best interest. A.J. feels the same. There will be a lot of bumps in the road in life. They want to prove to themselves that giving up is never a good option," Mr. Spechler said.

"What the hell do they know? They're just kids for Christ's sake. They are white kids surrounded by a bunch of spics and niggers who have no regard for human life," Kyle said.

"I've had just about enough of your bigoted mouth, Kyle. When people like you realize that all people of color, rich or poor, are human beings, we will all be a lot better off. For God's sake,

I can't believe Logan grew up hearing this nonsense and turned out to be the great kid he is," Arthur said.

Lilly reached out and put her hand on her husband's forearm to settle him down.

"How dare you, Arthur? Just because my husband doesn't sound politically correct like you do, doesn't mean he doesn't love his children," Kathy Darby said.

"Okay, okay. Let's all settle down for a minute. There is a lot of emotion running here. Mr. Darby, your choice of words is a bit surprising to me, but you have the absolute right to speak your mind under the circumstances. All I ask is that you...all of you, keep an open mind and think about what this program means to A.J., Logan, and millions of kids who are both privileged and disenfranchised in our society. Just keep an open mind, please. Look, I can't sit here and guarantee your children's safety any more than I could have guaranteed the safety of the kids who were murdered at Columbine or Sandy Hook. I might remind you all it was white kids who pulled the triggers on those guns; it could have easily happened here in Ridgewood High School," Mr. Spechler said. He tossed his pen on the desk in front of him, awaiting a response from the parents.

Kyle Darby's face was beet red with anger. He put his head down and thought for a moment. Kyle took a deep breath and exhaled slowly.

"Arthur, Lilly, Kathy, I apologize. Mr. Spechler, you are one hundred percent correct. I was way out of line with my language. Logan is a man, not a boy. We raised him to be a man and not run away from a problem. Based on what the police and the professionals at the school said, I think we can live with Logan's decision," Kyle said.

"You are indeed a good man, Kyle. I think I had you pegged wrong, and I, too, apologize if I offended you. I'm no better than you because I am more liberal in my thinking. God knows I have my moments. You have the right to speak your mind. Let's all go to the Park West Tavern and grab a beer. Maybe we could get to know each other a bit better," Arthur said.

"I'll ask my wife to join us," Ron Spechler said. He sensed his program was already working.

CHAPTER 23

07450

SHOWDOWN IN RIDGEWOOD

Mrs. Taylor picked Semaj and Rosa up at the usual time after school at the high school circle. Semaj ran to the car; Rosa was already sitting in the front seat of the shining, just detailed, Range Rover.

"Hey, Semaj. Hope your day was great!" Mrs. Taylor said.

"The best! I'm swamped with homework," Semaj replied.

"Rosa and I have something to do so we'll drop you off, and you can have at it."

"Cool, I'll see you guys later?" Semaj asked. *Where could they be going?* Semaj asked himself.

"Yes, of course. We'll be home before dinner. Mr. Taylor will not be joining us. He has a dinner meeting in the city, so it's just the three of us," Mrs. Taylor announced.

Semaj was dropped off at the house, and off Rosa and Mrs. Taylor proceeded to Rosa's first, personal trainer visit.

"Here is a chocolate, energy drink, Rosa. I'll prepare one every time you work out. It's important not to starve yourself and you must keep your energy level up. Then after the workout, you'll have a fruit smoothie at the club. Mrs. Taylor said. "Oh, and by the way, I got you a present. Cool work out clothes. I hope you like them."

"That's so nice of you, Mrs. Taylor, I was wondering what I was going to wear. I packed an old Clinton sweatshirt in my bag."

"I have you scheduled with my trainer for three times a week. I'm so excited for you!" Mrs. Taylor said.

Rosa's work out took an hour. She and Mrs. Taylor hung out at the gym for a while, sipping their drinks and chatting about nutrition and school.

I love this woman. I wish my mom was like her in some ways, Rosa thought.

After dinner, Rosa and Semaj helped load the dishwasher. Rosa motioned with her head to Semaj. She wanted to see him upstairs.

The two boarders went to Rosa's room.

"You said you needed to talk, what's up?" Semaj asked.

"You are the talk of the senior class, Semaj. Have you heard the gossip?"

"No, what gossip?"

ZIP CODE

"Evidently, your new BFF Nicole has been telling her friends that you and she have hooked up."

"What? You're kidding right?" Semaj bellowed.

"No, I'm not kidding. Dude, don't you see what she's doing?"

"No, I'm blown away!"

"Semaj, she is the most bitchy girl in the entire school. You're just a trophy to her. A big, ebony statue she can parade around showing how cool and liberal she is. The heart throb of Ridgewood High School scored first with the boy from the ghetto," Rosa said. She seemed angry.

"You seem pissed at me."

"More disappointed. Nicole trapped you, and you were too dumb to see it coming, Semaj."

"She's really not like that."

"Oh, no? Then tell me what she is like then?" Rosa asked.

"We started out as friends. She's very smart and we had great talks. It was all cool."

"Yeah, she's smart like a Venus Flytrap. She lured you in, and now she will crush your skin and bones." Rosa sounded preachy.

"She's not prejudice. She doesn't see color. It's not about that. Not at all!" Semaj said.

"How does this affect the program? How will this make you look to the rest of the class? And what happens when the story gets to all the parents? They probably won't be so understanding about the boy toy image. I can't wait to see the prom pictures," Rosa declared.

"I think you're blowing this thing way out of proportion, Rosa," Semaj said. He was looking at Rosa with an incredulous glare. "Anyway, what was I supposed to do, just walk away?"

"I get it. It's hard for a man to think he is being taken advantage of. All I'm saying is you need to be careful. Rumors spread quickly. This could explode in your face, or it could wind up hurting you in more ways than you can imagine," Rosa advised.

"And what about you? If some dude came onto you, what would you do?" Semaj asked.

"This is not about me, dude. I don't have a reputation. Besides, with all these skinny girls around, all I get are polite smiles."

"Oh, so you're saying that because you're not all svelte, no guy will go near you? You must be kidding!"

"Is that the 'fat girls need loving, too?', macho bullshit?" Rosa asked.

"You're not fat, Rosa!"

"Well, for your information, and not that it's any of your business, Mrs. Taylor has me on a nutrition and exercise program. I asked her for help and if you breathe a word...."

ZIP CODE

Semaj interrupted, "Is your self esteem so low that you feel a need to cry out for help?"

"You are such an ass sometimes," Rosa said. *You're not fat, so what the hell do you know?* Rosa's thought brought tears to her eyes,

Semaj began singing a Bruno Mars song.

"Her lips, her lips, I could kiss them all day if she'd let me
Her laugh, her laugh, she hates, but I think it's so sexy,
She's so beautiful
And I tell her everyday

Oh, you know, you know, you know I'd never ask you to change
If perfect's what you're searching for, then just stay the same
So don't even bother asking if you look ok
You know I'll say

When I see you face
There's not a single thing I would change
'Cause you're amazing
Just the way you are

And when you smile
The whole world stops and stares for awhile
'Cause girl, you're amazing
Just the way you are"

"Semaj, don't! Don't make fun of me like that!" Rosa said, tears running down her face.

Semaj embraced Rosa. He began humming the song, leading her into a slow dance.

"I would never, ever do that to you, Rosa. You are the most incredible girl I've ever known."

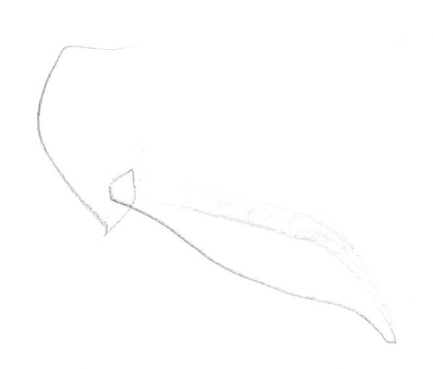

CHAPTER 24

Logan and A.J. were in only two classes together at DeWitt Clinton. One was the newly established, Urban Studies course, established by Mr. Taveleres. The Social Studies Department administered the course.

Mr. Paul Aaronson, a distinguished looking, retired, urban planner for the City of New York teaches the Urban Studies class.

In a three-piece gray, pin-striped suit, light blue, woven silk tie, and polished, black wingtip, oxford shoes, Mr. Aaronson looked more like an investment banker than a high school teacher. His demeanor was serious, but approachable.

"Urban planning back when I graduated college in the nineteen sixties was all about land use, transportation planning, architecture, and structuring communities. Today, due to urban renewal and the regeneration of inner cities, urban planning has become more about sustainability, the proper use of natural resources, pollution, climate change, and our biggest, national problem, in my view, growing social inequity.

So rather than study the Romans and how they planned their cities, as I was forced to do, I think we need to concentrate on social inequity and how we can affect change in our major cities, Who wants to kick off a discussion?" Mr. Aaronson asked the class of twenty-five students.

"Yes, in the back. Please state your name until I get a handle on everyone in the class," Aaronson said.

"I'm Keith Copeland, sir. It seems to me our society is not ready to adjust social inequity at the moment. I point to our current mayor. He is a liberal progressive. Every time I read or hear criticism of him, the words socialist or communist comes up in a negative light. Don't you think his timing may be a little bit off?" Keith asked. He looked at A.J. to see her reaction to his thoughts. A.J. continued taking notes, not making eye contact with Keith.

"Anyone?" Aaronson asked the class. "Yes, go ahead young man."

"Kenny Vazquez. I look at the Bronx for example. There has been a tremendous resurgence in building new, non-public housing here. I've seen photographs of entire neighborhoods which looked like they literally were bombed from the air. Like in the seventies and eighties. Entire blocks which were burned and only the shells of their structures remained. Those neighborhoods have been resurrected and rebuilt. A lot of the money for this development is federal, so it looks to me that things are a lot better, at least in the Bronx anyway," Kenny said.

"Good point. You are all too young to remember that blight. It was an amazing decline. Things do appear to have improved," Aaronson said. "Let's continue, good observations so far. Who else?"

"I'm Junior, I mean Papo Diaz. New apartments which are mostly government subsidized have not improved the unemployment situation among Blacks and Latinos. Isn't that where social inequity really needs to be reformed? Jobs for the lower class?" Papo "Junior" Diaz said.

"Lamar Butler, sir. Until the white folks get used to the fact that they have to share the wealth, we are doomed in the inner cities. The rich, white Republicans do everything they can to prevent redistribution of wealth. It's like we have two different countries," Lamar added.

A.J. cleared her throat and raised her hand.

"Go ahead." Aaronson pointed to A.J.

"Alexandra Taylor. As you can see, I'm white, and yes my family and I are basically Republicans. Why does that make it our job to give away what my father and mother have worked so hard for? I agree with Junior that employment must improve among minorities. All we hear is how much lower the unemployment rate is today under the current Obama administration. All I see around these neighborhoods are men and women hanging out and not working. Taking welfare and food stamps are not the answer. Working is far better for the future development of our cities, in my opinion," A.J stated.

"That's way easy for you to say. The only Hispanics you ever see are mowing your lawn. Blacks delivering furniture and appliances," Lamar said.

"But they're working. Not hanging out drinking beer and smoking dope. Sorry, I'm Logan...Logan Darby."

"And not getting anywhere by working. Sometimes they can make more on welfare and food stamps and making babies. To you, that's communism," Keith added.

"Look, it was capitalism that made this country great. Things like social security from FDR's presidency, and Medicare during the Johnson administration. Of course, we are, to some degree, socialistic, but necessary," A.J. said.

"Yeah, those presidents were both Democrats, by the way. The Democrats feel for the poor. Not you republicans. And Medicare will probably not be there for any of us anyway," Keith responded.

"So how do we build up our inner cities? Where do we get the money? Tax the people who have it! Take more and more away from people who have worked for what they have. That builds up a lot of resentment in the white community," Logan said.

A black student stood up and interrupted the discussion.

"And we have built up a resentment for being put in chains by your ancestors. Plain and simple."

"Sorry, I didn't get your name?" Aaronson asked.

"William Reynolds, the Third. Yes sir, that was the slave name of my people. Reynolds. Massa Reynolds owned the rice plantation in Myrtle Beach, South Carolina where we were bought and sold. Now it's a golf playground for mostly white people, and many of us are still shuckin' and jivin' to white authority, " William said.

"Look, don't look at all whites as slave owners. My great-great-grandfather came from Ireland in the eighteen forties to avoid starvation. My people were treated poorly when they arrived. For decades and decades after they got here they worked for pennies to just get by. Not one of us took a nickel of welfare. And that was what. Let me do the math for you, eighteen forty from sixteen nineteen…two hundred and twenty one years. And three hundred and ninety six years later you are still using slavery as a crutch. Just stop it!" A.J. said.

ZIP CODE

"Oooooo, she told you, brother!" someone said.

"Okay, lets settle down a bit. I'm so proud of the students who participated in this discussion. I want to continue it next session and hear from others how they feel about the topic. I'm going to break you up in random groups for the next month. You will have reading assignments to fulfill and tests will be graded on the text. The groups will form their own plan for urban planning. Which seemingly has become a euphemism for social inequity. You will also be graded by your group's presentation. Until next time," Aaronson said.

Keith caught up to A.J. as she was walking to her next class. Logan went in his own direction.

"Hey A.J., what's up? You mad at me or something?" Keith asked.

"About our discussion just now? Don't be silly."

"Nah, not about class. I texted you like twenty times and tried to call you since Saturday night. No texts back, and your phone always goes into your message box."

"Look Keith, I'm not interested in dating anyone right now. Being friends at school is fine, but that's where I want it to stay, A.J. said. She looked straight ahead, never making eye contact, like she learned on the streets and in the subway.

"I guess the color thing is an issue for you," Keith said.

"I don't care if you are polka-dot or green. Color means nothing to me. I just don't want a relationship at the moment. I have more pressing things to be concerned about. Let's just stay the way it is, classmates."

"Okay, that's cool. See you later." Keith said. *Stuck up, white bitch,* is what he thought.

CHAPTER 25

The morning after Rosa told Semaj about the scurrilous gossip which was traveling around the school with his name all over it, Semaj was walking to his first class when another senior, a star, football player for the Maroons and two of his buddies, passed him in the hallway.

"Hey, study man. Why don't you tell us all about it? That's what we do around here, ya know. Kiss and tell!" the jock said. His friends made kissing sounds mocking Semaj.

Semaj gave them a smirk and kept walking. Rosa was right. The word was out about his hookup with Nicole. *Dammit. Now what?* Semaj thought.

A few minutes later Semaj received a text from Nicole:

> Hi, ya! Guess what? Parents won't be home 2nite. Let's hang at my house. Pick u up after school. Kisses XXX

Immediately, Semaj texted one word back to Nicole:

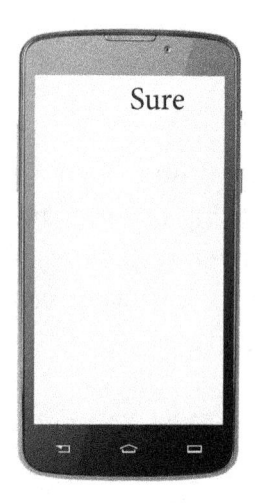

Sure

Throughout the day, Semaj was getting paranoid. A couple of girls giggled when they passed him in the library. One of the male seniors made an obscene gesture intending Semaj to see it in the cafeteria. He passed Nicole during they day and she blew him a kiss in front of some of her friends.

A part of Semaj was proud of his conquest. A part of him was feeling vanquished. He kept hearing Rosa's words. *You are a trophy, an ebony statue.*

Sweet Jesus, give me strength. The flesh is weak, Lord, Semaj said to himself.

Semaj texted Mrs. Taylor to tell her he wouldn't need to be picked up and was eating out with friends.

ZIP CODE

Rosa was invited to go to the mall right after school. *Going to the mall with Steph and Michelle after school. I'll be home in time for dinner. I have an apple...lol,* Rosa texted Mrs. Taylor.

The girls went to the Garden State Plaza. They stopped at Starbucks for coffee and a snack. Steph and Michelle shared a scone. Rosa munched on her apple. As they were walking toward the stores, a couple of older, rough looking Hispanic boys approached Rosa.

"Mommie chula, eso es todo tuyo? Arroz que carne hay. You looking fine," one of the thugs said.

The other guy had a smug face and chimed in, "*Todo esa curva y yo sin freno.*"

"I'm not your mommie. *Vete al carajo,*" Rosa replied as she walked away with the girls.

"What the heck was that?" Michelle asked.

"Just two pigs."

"What did you say to them?" Steph asked.

"Oh, nothing. I just told them to go to hell," Rosa replied.

"Mall creeps. It's getting worse by the day," Michelle said.

"No, really, what did they say to you, Rosa?" Steph asked.

"Well it's no secret that Spanish men like more meat on their women. The first guy asked me if all this was all mine. Then he said serve the rice because there's a lot of meat. The second jerk said there are a lot of curves and he has no brakes," Rosa replied.

"What friggin' animals!" Michelle wailed.

"Not really, that's pretty standard where I come from," Rosa replied.

Michelle needed to get some new leggings and Steph needed another pair of shoes. They headed for the mall entrance of Nordstrom's.

"More shoes, Steph? You're a shoe freak. How many shoes do you have anyway?" Michelle asked.

"I have no idea. Fifty, sixty, who even knows? A girl can never have enough shoes, you know," Steph laughed.

"Let me get the leggings first, so we can all try on some shoes. Maybe I'll get that pair of short boots I need," Michelle said.

"Are you into shoes, Rosa?" Steph asked.

"I'm more into fruit at the moment. I started a nutritional and exercise program. No shoes for me!" Rosa announced. She laughed and so did Michelle and Steph.

Michelle tried on a dozen leggings. She modeled them for Rosa and Steph, asking how she looked in each pair. She looked fantastic in all of them. She decided on three different pair. Two in black, one in beige. The beige pair had slits on the calves.

I would look like a cow in those, Rosa thought.

ZIP CODE

Michelle opened her *Louis Vuitton* handbag and took out her dad's Platinum American Express card. The cashier didn't even ask for her ID. Price was not even considered. *That bag is like three months rent for my mom. No way it's a knockoff,* Rosa said to herself.

Off to the shoe department they went. *Gucci, Versace, Jimmy Choo, Prada...*Michelle and Steph tried on endless pairs of boots and shoes.

The carnage of shoes, empty shoeboxes, tissue paper, and soft, monogrammed carry bags for the shoes littered the entire area where the girls sat. The obviously gay salesman ran quickly back and forth to the stockroom. Michelle said he was adorable. Steph thought he looked like Matt Damon.

Rosa kept her feet under the chair in which she was sitting, pretending to enjoy the melee. She was too self-conscious about her ten and a half shoe size. *The one thing I inherited from my father, boats for feet!* Rosa lamented to herself.

No prices were considered, and the Matt Damon kid never offered. Rosa was flabbergasted. Out came the Platinum cards. Each girl signed for the pair of shoes they each purchased.

Note to self: No more shopping with these girls. I don't belong here unless I take a job as a Christmas wrapper, Rosa laughed to herself.

�֎

Back at *Tall Pines*, Nicole grabbed two beers and headed for the great room with Semaj.

"Hold it, Nic. I can't show up at the Taylor's smelling of beer. How about a Coke?" Semaj said.

"Sure, in the fridge behind the bar. I'll do these two myself," Nicole said. She chugged the first *Heineken*, draining the bottle like a thirsty, farm hand.

"No music this time," Nicole said. She made her move on Semaj. She had no inhibitions.

Semaj was defenseless.

ZIP CODE

CHAPTER 26

Being in high school, anywhere is a challenge that is not for the faint of heart. Academic pressure, social issues, dating, sports, part time jobs, problems at home, parents splitting up or already divorced, a parent who just lost his or her job, death of a grandparent or other relative. The list is endless. The burden is enormous.

Ron Spechler recognized that the social aspect of his program would be the most troublesome for the four students involved. He also was aware the families that were part of his bold experiment would need a time out.

The plan was to have each student return home for a weekend at week four. Spechler's grandmother, his *boobie,* often told him in Yiddish, *'Der mentsh traknt un got lakht,'* Man plans and God laughs. Sure enough, on what was to be the back-to-home weekend, twenty-six inches of snow blanketed the New York metropolitan area.

So it was five weeks before the parents and friends of the four participants would see each other. Sonia picked up Delores Henry, Semaj's mom to drive A.J. and Logan back to Ridgewood. Arthur and Lilly Taylor drew straws with the Darbys. They took Semaj and Rosa back to the Bronx. The families would be reunited that Friday night in their respective homes and stay for the short weekend.

When Sonia and Mrs. Henry reached May as Well, A.J.'s home, they were blown away at the opulence which surrounded them.

"Sweet baby Jesus, look at this place. It's out of a fairy tale," Mrs. Henry said.

"Breathtaking," was the only word Sonia could think of.

A.J. took the two mothers on a tour of the estate.

People actually have this kind of money? Sonia thought.

"Hold on, babies, I need to take a few pictures for my church group. They will never believe my words," Delores said.

Mrs. Taylor prepared some food for the kids and the moms and left the offering on the kitchen's center island.

"My, my, my...look at this spread. It could feed my entire assembly at the church," Delores added.

Wait until till they see the dump we live in, Sonia said to herself.

A.J., Logan, and the two Bronx ladies enjoyed the food while looking out of the kitchen's bay window. As if on queue, a family of deer appeared in the back yard. The elegantly, tamed animal family ate from a selection of treats the Taylors kept for them on a small, wrought-iron table. The buck treated himself to the molasses and salt deer lick which hung from a nearby birch tree.

ZIP CODE

Logan said his goodbyes. Friends from school picked him up at A.J.'s place and brought him home to *Tall Oaks*.

After an hour, Sonia and Delores headed back to the Bronx. They were slammed in the usual bumper-to-bumper traffic on the George Washington Bridge and the Cross Bronx Expressway.

"Our kids are certainly seeing what the other half lives like. I've never seen a place like that," Sonia said.

"And they even have a name for the home. I'm gonna name my place too. Something like, *Peeling Paint* suits it just fine," Delores said. The two ladies laughed hysterically. They went back and forth with possible names for their apartments.

Roach Heaven, Chilly Winds, Smelly Hallways, on and on, each name bringing out belly laughs.

Arthur Taylor pulled his gleaming, green Jaguar XJ alongside 749 Fox Street in the Bronx.

Good-bye car, you were fun, Arthur thought as he and Lilly walked Rosa and Semaj up to the apartment.

Lilly's eyes were as large as tea saucers as she took in the neighborhood.

Rosa used her keys to open the bottom lock and the iron barred police lock to the apartment.

"Home, sweet home," Rosa said.

Lilly's mouth went dry.

"How long have you and your mom lived here, Rosa?" Arthur asked.

"Oh, since I was a baby. Mom lived here forever. It's rent controlled," Rosa said.

As if on cue, a large cockroach walked up the kitchen wall.

Lilly felt faint.

They took a minute to tour the apartment. That was all they needed.

"Okay, kids, we'll see you on Sunday. I'm bringing A.J. and Logan back here, and we'll take you guys back with me," Arthur said.

Over my dead body, Lilly thought.

CHAPTER 27

While A.J. stayed at home and waited for her mom and dad to return from the Bronx, she made phone calls and texted her friends to make plans for later that night and Saturday.

Logan hit the ground running. Instead of going home, two of his friends, both fellow Ridgewood Crew members picked him up. They decided to run over to the Paramus Park Mall to hang out and see who they could meet up with. Namely, girls from Immaculate Heart Academy, ZIP CODE 07646 or Holy Angels, ZIP CODE 07627. Both schools are in affluent towns in Bergen County, New Jersey.

"Okay Loge, we want details," Bobby Clarke said.

"Dude, you like stopped texting about you and that Spanish girl. Tell us all the smoky details," Lenny DeSanto added.

"I'm in enough hot water as it is. It's turned into a nightmare for me. I told you guys too much already," Logan said.

"Dude, it's just us. We won't say a word to anyone," Lenny said.

"Hey, by the way. Have you heard about Nicole and that Semaj dude? They're doing more than homework together!" Bobby added.

"Yeah, word travels fast. She's gross. I think she's been with half the football team," Logan said.

"She has a new nickname," Lenny stated.

"I can't wait for this one," Logan replied.

"Mrs. Robinson. Get it? She broke the color barrier," Bobby chimed in.

"Grow up!" Logan felt like he was back in seventh grade.

"Dude, back to you. You could have been stabbed, shot, tortured who knows what?" Bobby said.

"It's all cool. Let's just change the subject, okay?" Logan asked.

"Later tonight we'll get you to talk after five or six brewskis," Lenny said.

"How are those two kids from the Bronx doing, anyway?" Logan asked.

"Semaj is doing better than the three of us!" Bobby quipped.

"Seriously?" Logan said.

"He's a good guy. Really smart! He doesn't talk like the rest of the blacks. He's not even into rap, if you can even believe that!" Lenny said.

"Does he also like chicken and watermelon? Really, Len? Maybe I've been away too long," Logan stated.

ZIP CODE

"This whole Bronx thing made you lose your sense of humor, bro," Lenny said.

"Nah, it just opened my eyes about some things."

"Dude, you opened your zipper too!" Bobby said. He and Lenny burst out laughing.

Logan rolled his eyes.

A bit later, Arthur and Lilly Taylor arrived back at their home in Ridgewood. A.J. heard the garage door open and ran to greet her parents.

They were all thrilled to see each other. Hugs and kisses were passed all around. Lilly Taylor wiped tears from her eyes.

"Oh mom! What will you do when I go to Columbia?"

"I may come with you! Here, let me look at you."

Lilly looked at her daughter from head to foot as if she were checking for stab wounds or gunshots.

"Mom, I'm fine! Really, fine! Dad, please tell her I'm fine!"

"She's fine, Lil," Arthur complied.

"We need to talk, sweetie. Let's go upstairs. I think I need a drink," Lilly said.

"Mom, you don't really drink!" A.J. said.

"I may start tonight," Lilly announced.

"Just go easy on her. I think she's traumatized," Arthur whispered to his daughter.

Up in the kitchen, Lilly poured herself a large orange juice. Arthur made himself a real drink. Johnny Walker Black on the rocks. A.J. just sat at the table. It seems the kitchen is the place for all family discussions, no matter what the income level.

"Okay, I have to get right to the point A.J. You know I'm not one to mince words. How in hell can you live in that place? I want you not to go back!" Lilly asked and answered her own question.

"Mom, stop. It's a little rough, but that's part of the program. We're learning so much, it's utterly amazing," A.J. said.

"A little rough? I'm going through your bag before you unpack to inspect for cockroaches and other vermin. Arthur, I want you to call the pest control people in the morning. Maybe they have a twenty-four hour service, call now!"

"Lil, please, you're getting really carried away."

"Mom, agreed, it is what it is, but I will not quit because you saw a cockroach and a tiny apartment. It's all a learning process for me. The program has already helped define me as a well-rounded person. Ridgewood is fabulous and I'm grateful to you and dad for what you provided, really I am. Please relax and keep an open mind," A.J. said.

"That whole thing with Logan had me up for nights with worry," Lilly choked back tears.

"That's behind us. We both learned from that."

"A.J. we will support you one-hundred percent. But that's not to say I will not be there dragging you out of that apartment, kicking and screaming if we believe you are in immanent danger," Arthur said.

"So, what's for dinner?" A.J. asked. She wanted to change the subject.

"I thought we would go to the Allendale Bar and Grill. Dad loves the steak, and we can have the Dover Sole."

"Great, I'm starved. After dinner I would like to go out with the girls. My phone has about twenty texts, and a gazillion questions."

After dinner, A.J. and her friends met on East Ridgewood Avenue at a new jazz Café. The questions flew at her from every direction.

"Tell us about the subways, are they dangerous? Has anyone hit on you at Clinton? Are there any other white kids? What really happened with Logan and that Spanish girl...no what REALLY happened? That pizza looked amazing, was it that good? How is it going to a school with so many thugs? Do they only listen to Hip-Hop? Who are their favorite performers? Are there really creepy-crawly bugs where you live? What do you think about Nicole? Are you going back?"

A.J. answered all questions like she was at a press conference. When it came to Logan, the girls didn't get what they wanted to hear.

CHAPTER 28

The weekend went by like a flash. The students were all back in their adopted homes and ready to begin the school week.

Semaj had texted Nicole several times over the weekend. Her responses back to him were short, curt, and a few times she didn't bother to answer.

Semaj saw Nicole before homeroom on Monday morning.

"Hey, Nic, what's up?"

"How was your weekend?" Nicole responded with a chill in her voice.

"It was quick. Good to get home, though. Saw some friends and hung out a bit. It was too cold to do much else. How was yours?"

"Fine. It was cold here, too."

"Nic, what's up with you? You seem pissed for some reason."

"I'm sure you were with your ghetto girlfriend. You didn't even bother to call me."

"I texted you like twenty times. And there is no ghetto girl as you put it."

"You could have at least called me, Semaj!"

"Sorry, next time I will."

"There may not be a next time."

Semaj paused. He heard Rosa's voice in his head.

"What's that supposed to mean?" Semaj asked.

"Look, Semaj. What we had was just a fling. It's time to move on."

"Is that how it is? The entire senior class knows about us. That had to come from you, girl. I don't kiss and tell."

"Whatever!" Nicole said, dismissing Semaj quickly.

"So you just wanted a conquest. Apparently I was the victim."

"Just like your people, you have a persecution complex."

"My people? My people? I guess I'm just part of the narrative in your world. Suddenly it's a black thing?" Semaj asked. There was a fury in his eyes.

"Be honest, Semaj. There was never a future for us. Grow up and get over it."

"A future?"

"Semaj, I'm just living in the here and now. It is what it is."

ZIP CODE

"So you scored with the black, ghetto kid. I'm just another trophy for your family room mantle piece, I suppose."

"Deal with it. Lose my number!" Nicole blurted. She said those words loud enough to be heard by anyone standing nearby. She walked out of homeroom to add to the drama.

A few of the kids sitting around the classroom pretended to be looking at their cell phones. Semaj felt the sting of embarrassment.

In the cafeteria, Semaj saw Rosa and her friends sitting at one of the round tables having their lunch. All the girls were using their cell phones rather than talking with each other.

Spoiled brats! They get to use their precious phones 24-7, Semaj thought.

Rosa saw Semaj and left the table.

"I just got summarily executed," Semaj said.

"I heard."

"Word gets around here pretty fast."

"Nicole's like a bee. Now she will go to the next flower," Rosa said. She felt terrible for her friend.

"It wasn't as if you didn't tell me, Rosa."

"Just put it behind you. I'm sure you learned something from this."

"Yeah, like everything else in life, the hard way," Semaj lamented.

"Hey, me and the girls are going into town after school. Mich has to go to the store to pick something up. I don't have a workout scheduled until tomorrow. Why don't you come with us?" Rosa asked.

"Sure, I don't want to mope all day feeling sorry for myself."

"Great, I'll text Mrs. Taylor."

As planned, Michelle, Steph, Rosa, and Semaj went into downtown Ridgewood right after school ended. They all had their Vento-Grande lattes, Smoked Butterscotch for Michelle, a Frappuccino for Steph, and a Fizzio soda for Semaj. Rosa chose a black coffee with the Stevia sweetener Mrs. Taylor had given to her.

They headed over to Ridgewood Jewelers. Michelle was looking for a pair of much-needed gold, hoop earrings. A few other girls from school saw the group inside the store from the street and walked in to add to the confusion.

ZIP CODE

The lady behind the counter laid out a few selections for Michelle. She held the jewelry up to her ear, looked into a counter mirror, and then modeled them for the group. The sales lady was called to another counter and left it to the small crowd to help Michelle make her selection.

"So have you decided on a pair?" The sales lady asked when she returned.

"I don't see anything I really like at the moment," Michelle politely said.

As she started to put the selections back into the glass case, the students began to walk out of the store.

"Hold on a second. There were five sets of earrings that I left out. There are only four here," the lady said.

The rest of the girls had already left the store, leaving Michelle, Rosa, Semaj, and Steph, who walked back to the counter.

The whole time the sales lady kept looking at Semaj.

The owner of the store walked up to the group from behind the counter joining the frantic sales lady.

"Is there a problem?" the owner asked.

"Well, I took out five pair of earrings for this young lady to look at, and when I returned to the counter only four were here," the sales lady stated.

The owner looked right at Semaj, ignoring the three girls. The girls began looking at the floor for the missing set.

"Okay kids, just put the pair on the counter and call it a day," the owner said, still looking directly at Semaj.

"Are you kidding me, right now?" Michelle said.

"No, I'm not kidding. This kind of old scam doesn't work around here. Just return the set before I am forced to call the police."

Semaj felt his face go flush.

"Listen, mister, we didn't take your earrings, okay?" Rosa blurted. A tinge of Bronx Latina accent came out, surprising everyone.

The police were called. Within minutes, two Ridgewood patrolmen entered the store. They asked what had happened and were told the situation by the store owner. Both police officers looked at Semaj.

"Dude, I didn't take the jewelry," Semaj said.

"Why would he take the earrings? We weren't the only ones standing here in the first place!" Steph said.

One of the officers took Semaj by the arm and walked him a few feet away from the group. He asked Semaj's name, address and date of birth, and jotted the information onto a small notebook.

Semaj complied, giving his Bronx home address.

"Look, if you have the stuff, just tell me now and we can forget the whole thing," the cop said.

ZIP CODE

"I don't have them, officer. I don't steal. That's not me," Semaj responded.

"Stay right here."

The officer went out to his patrol car while the other policeman stayed with the group.

"He didn't take the jewelry. What is it, because he's the only black kid you ever saw?" Michelle said to the store owner.

"That's enough, miss. Just be quiet. We will get to the bottom of this," the policeman interrupted.

Semaj stood where he was told and put his hands on his hips, shaking his head in disbelief.

The officer returned to the store. A plainclothes detective had just arrived and walked in with him. Rosa texted Mrs. Taylor. *We are in Ridgewood Jewelers. They are accusing Semaj of stealing.*

"You have no priors, young man. That's a good thing. But I'm afraid I'm going to have to search you, so please turn around and put your hands against the wall. I'm not arresting you at this point, so I don't have to read you your rights."

"He has no rights...he's black!" Michelle hollered.

"That will be enough out of you, young lady. Just let us do our job here, and everyone can go home."

"I can say anything I want. You guys storm in here and the first person you blame is him. What about me? What about these two standing next to me? What about the girls who were here and left? This is so unfair!" Michelle said.

"Yeah, why don't you go find them, and search the three of us too? This is nonsense; I'm calling my dad," Steph said.

Rosa started to cry. She wasn't afraid. She was angry.

"What seems to be the problem here, officer?" Lilly Taylor entered the store. She had been a block away at the butcher shop.

"Oh, hello, Mrs. Taylor. Do you know this young man?" the officer asked.

"Indeed I do. He and this young woman are staying at my home for the semester. What's going on?" Mrs. Taylor asked.

The officer explained the situation and the accusation.

"We need to do a quick search of the young man. He's eighteen so he can be charged as an adult if he has stolen the items," the officer said.

"Give me a minute, please," Mrs. Taylor said to the policeman. She walked over to Semaj who was looking more and more angry.

"Don't you see what's happening here, Mrs. Taylor? They right away blame Semaj. And for only one reason!" Michelle said.

"I'll handle this Michelle, just relax," Mrs. Taylor said.

Mrs. Taylor went close to Semaj.

ZIP CODE

"Semaj, did you steal the earrings? Just tell me if you have them or not."

"No ma'am, I did not," Semaj stated.

"That's good enough for me," Mrs. Taylor announced loud enough for everyone to hear. She turned to the two, uniformed policemen. The detective went to the back office of the store with the owner.

"Officers, you have no probable cause to detain or search this boy. If he said he didn't steal the jewelry, he didn't steal it. I will not abide his being profiled."

"Excuse me, Mrs. Taylor. Son, you are free to go. I'm sorry for any misunderstanding," the detective said. He had returned to the counter with the store owner. They had reviewed the store's surveillance cameras. One of the girls from the other group had palmed the earrings.

"Let's go, kids. Rosa, Semaj, I'll take you home. Officers, I'm sorry, but you should all be ashamed of yourselves. This is no way to treat someone because of the color of his or her skin. You haven't heard the end of this," Mrs. Taylor said. She was furious.

LOUIS ROMANO

CHAPTER 29

Early that evening, after the drama at the jewelry store, and a long conversation with Rosa and Semaj, Lilly Taylor was spent. The extra-lean, center cut, pork chops she purchased at the butcher shop would go uncooked.

Arthur Taylor arrived at the normal time from his day at the office. There was no normal aroma of a home cooked meal coming from the kitchen. He called out that he was home to no response. Rosa and Semaj were laying low in Rosa's room texting away to their friends, both in the Bronx and Ridgewood, while listening to their own music on personal ear buds.

By six o'clock that evening, not only the senior class had been alerted to the jewelry store story, the entire school was abuzz. Mr. Spechler heard about it from one of the guidance counselors. He called Semaj and they discussed briefly how the event was totally unfortunate.

"Hang in there, Semaj. We all love you!"

"Stupid cops. They suck!"

"Prejudice in any form is just ignorance. We are all behind you dude."

"So sorry for this Semaj. We all don't think like that."

Dozens of texts like these made Semaj an instant, school celebrity. Unlike the Nicole situation, the student body rallied around their transferred, Clinton classmate.

Semaj's phone kept buzzing like mad.

Arthur made his way to his bedroom suite. He found Lilly sitting in the darkened room. She had been crying.

"Lil, honey, what's wrong? Are you okay?"

"Sorry, sweetie. I just couldn't bring myself to prepare dinner."

"What the heck happened?" Arthur asked.

Lilly hugged her husband tightly and began a fresh cry.

After composing herself, Lilly told her husband about the event of the day.

"Lil, you handled it brilliantly. So why are you so upset? You normally don't break down like this."

"Sweetie, it's not what happened to Semaj. Yes, his being singled out unfairly was upsetting. Those men had no right to accuse him of being a thief. No right at all to single him out. You need to talk to the mayor and the police chief. These men should be reprimanded."

"You still haven't told me why you're so emotional," Arthur said.

"Do you remember the day before Rosa and Semaj came to stay with us? All we knew is that a black and a Puerto Rican student were coming here. That's all we knew."

"Okay...and?"

"And we took all of our expensive jewelry, your watches, all of my bracelets and necklaces, and my mom's wedding rings, and we hid them in the wall safe. Arthur, we are no better than those policemen. We didn't even know these great kids, yet we assumed they were thieves. Giving them the alarm code was bogus. What could they steal, my dresses? A flat screen TV?"

"We were just being cautious, Lil. That's all," Arthur said

"We were being bigoted, plain and simple. We are no better than anyone else who has extreme prejudice."

"I see your point, I guess. But we didn't want to put any temptation..."

"C'mon, will you. It wasn't about temptation at all. We both know why we hid the expensive stuff. I'm so ashamed of myself for thinking that way," Lilly interrupted.

"Where are the kids now? Let's go over to *Greek To Me* in town and have a quick dinner. I'm starved, they must be, too. C'mon, Lil," Arthur offered.

They all climbed into Lilly's Range Rover for the five-minute ride to the family restaurant.

Nothing was mentioned about the incident on the ride over.

"I love the Gyro here. And the garlic-lemon fries are killer," Arthur said.

"Sounds good to me!" Semaj agreed.

"Rosa and I will make good choices. You guys can clog up your arteries all you want," Lilly said. They all laughed.

"What do you think, Rosa?" Lilly asked.

Looking at the menu, Rosa made her decision.

"How about the grilled chicken, Greek salad?" Rosa asked.

"Me, too! Perfect! Plain vinegar on the side, no cheese?" Lilly responded.

"Cool!" Rosa smiled.

The waitress took their orders.

Sitting at a table on the other side of the restaurant was the Chief of Police, Mike Grabowski and his wife. The chief excused himself and walked over to the Taylors' table.

"Arthur, Lillian, long-time, no see," Grabowski said.

Arthur stood and shook the chief's hand with both of his. Lilly smiled and said hello. Rosa and Semaj had no idea who the man was.

"You know how the winters are around here Mike; we all hibernate. How are things? Oh, by the way, please meet Semaj

ZIP CODE

Henry and Rosa Colon. They are studying at Ridgewood for the semester. They are our house guests."

Semaj and Rosa both stood and greeted the chief with firm handshakes and the standard, "nice to meet you" greeting.

"Mr. Grabowski is the Chief of Police of Ridgewood," Lilly stated.

Semaj swallowed hard. Rosa looked down at her glass of ice water on the red-checkered table.

"Yes, I know. I know who these fine students are. That's one of the reasons I came over here. May I sit for a minute?"

"Delighted!" Arthur said.

Grabowski pulled a chair over from an adjacent table.

"Semaj, I want to officially apologize, from me and my entire department for what happened to you today. I think we all may have learned a lesson."

"Thank-you, sir. It was just a misunderstanding," Semaj said.

Yeah, my butt, Rosa said to herself.

"I understand you were a perfect gentleman. Things could have escalated if you behaved differently," Grabowski said.

"So who took the earrings?" Rosa blurted.

"I really can't say that, Rosa. I can tell you the items were returned after the parents were called. She's a minor so it has to stay confidential. I'm sure you understand."

"Mike, you are the best. Coming over here was a nice thing to do for all of us. Where is your lovely wife, Ruth?" Arthur asked.

"She's gonna holler at me. She's over there, her *Pasticcio* is getting cold."

"Can she come over to say hi for a sec?" Lilly asked.

The Chief caught his wife's attention and waved for her to come to the Taylors' table.

Ruth Grabowski smiled widely and walked over to the table. Her husband, Arthur, and Semaj rose from their chairs to greet her.

Semaj almost fell to the floor.

Ruth Grabowski is black.

CHAPTER 30

The days on the calendar flew by. Both A.J. and Logan were becoming the most popular kids in the class. Largely because they are really just regular kids, in spite of their advantageous zip code. Down to earth, no pretense, easy to talk to, and always willing to help their fellow students.

Both A.J. and Logan started study groups and also tutored in Math and English. Anyone who needed special attention on any subject simply had to reach out by text, and appointments were made.

Luie Morales was having a tough time with AP Calculus. A.J. showed him an easy way to study, and he aced an important mid-term. He offered A.J. a ten-dollar bill for her time.

"Luie, would you charge me if I needed help?" A.J. asked.

"Well...well no I wouldn't," Luie replied.

"So why would you think I would take money from you or any other friend or student? We are all in this together, Luie."

One day, as the winter weather began to subside, Logan was asked to play in a pick-up basketball game after school. A.J. had a study group that she was leading. The group met in Clinton's library which was not nearly as technologically sophisticated as Ridgewood High's. But it was quiet.

Logan texted A.J. literally as soon as the study group sat down.

"Hey, twisted my ankle a bit. Want to get back and ice it up. You almost ready?"

"OUCH!!! I'll be fine. We've taken that trip a hundred times. I'm right behind you."

Logan thought about Sonia's admonition never to be separated, but the traveling to and from school from Fox Street had become second nature. He decided to go back to the apartment without A.J.

After the tutoring session was over, A.J. made her way to the Jerome Avenue/ Mosholu Parkway elevated train station. She felt a bit strange going back to Fox Street alone, but was not the least bit nervous or apprehensive.

Dusk had begun to fall on the Bronx, and a blustering wind made A.J. remember it was still wintertime. She was longing for the spring and better weather.

The train ride was rote. Uneventful, same old same old. Everyone kept to themselves; some reading, some just staring ahead in a train trance waiting for their stop.

Transfer at 125th Street back up to the Bronx for the final leg of the forty-five minute trip. Hopefully, Sonia would be making some great Puerto Rican dinner. A.J. was famished from the long day.

ZIP CODE

A.J. exited the subway noticing the swirling wind had followed her home. What she didn't notice was the hooded thug who was following her since she got on the platform in Harlem.

He kept a reasonable distance in case his prey would look behind and see him more than once. A.J. never looked back, not even once. Her stalker picked up his pace, getting to within ten yards of A.J. He was walking along the curbside so as not to be seen following directly behind his victim.

A.J. turned onto Fox Street, nightfall had already arrived, the temperature dropping to near-freezing. A.J. brought her wool scarf closer to her chin to ward off the wind. The hooded perpetrator did not feel the elements. His adrenalin was pumping, as he anticipated his victim would soon be entering her building.

As A.J. alighted the few stairs to the Fox Street apartment house, her stalker walked past the entrance by a few yards, pivoted and bolted up the stairs just as A.J. was removing her key to the building's entrance door.

The thug pushed A.J into the dark corridor using her scarf to smother her cries for help. She was totally surprised by the attack. The large man brandished a long, switchblade knife he held in front of the shocked girl's eyes. A.J. felt her knees buckle as the maniac dragged her further into the empty lobby.

A.J. was dragged, like a small child down a staircase that led to the dark, dank basement.

"Drop the bag and shut your mouth or I'll cut your throat," the man said. "You will do exactly what I tell you or you will not see...."

The thug's sentence was interrupted with a smash to the back of his head. He fell to the ground like a sack of potatoes.

A.J. let out a blood-curdling scream. Sonia stood on top of the would-be assailant with her Glock sidearm pointed at his head. It was the gun that knocked the man senseless. Luckily for A.J., Sonia saw that man follow A.J. into the building. She was coming home to cook for her Ridgewood High School boarders.

"Please move. Please. Try to get up so I can end your miserable life right here," Sonia said to the man on the ground. The back of his head was bleeding onto the stairway.

The building superintendent hearing A.J.'s screams, came to the stairwell.

"Hey, what the hell is going on here?" The superintendent demanded.

"Jose, it's Sonia. Call 911. Tell them policeman needs assistance. Ten-Thirteen.

Within a minute, sirens were heard wailing as a platoon of police cars, both marked and unmarked came from both directions of Fox Street. Moments later, the building was swarming with NYPD's finest.

For good measure, Sonia gave the dirtbag another swat in the head with her gun. He was unconscious when other policeman came to Sonia's aid.

A.J. jumped over the man and into Sonia's arms.

ZIP CODE

"Are you okay, baby? Are you hurt? Did he cut you? Sonia asked. Sonia opened A.J.'s jacket to look for signs of blood.

"Oh, my God...Oh, my God!" A.J. said. That was all the poor girl could say before she fainted.

Two uniformed policemen and Sonia began to carry A.J. up the stairs. Logan was icing his twisted ankle and heard the commotion downstairs. He immediately thought of A.J. and ran down the stairs, meeting the police and A.J. as they headed for Sonia's apartment.

"What the hell happened?" a shocked Logan asked.

"She's alright. Just shaken up. We have an ambulance en route," one of the policemen responded.

"She'll be okay. If I were two minutes later, we could have had a tragedy. I'll deal with you later," Sonia said.

A.J. came to as she was being carried into the apartment. She had no idea where she was.

"Baby, just breathe, deep breaths, okay? Everything is fine. You are fine. If that piece of garbage had hurt you, I swear I would have shot him where he stood," Sonia said.

The New York Fire Department EMT team wanted to take A.J. to nearby Lincoln Hospital for observation from shock. She slowly gathered her strength and Sonia agreed she would be ok to stay home.

The man with the hoodie was unceremoniously thrown into a police cruiser and carted off to jail.

For the next hour, there were a half dozen, plain clothes detectives and uniformed cops in Sonia's apartment, taking notes and asking questions. A.J. barely remembered the attack. She could not identify the assailant. She never got a good look at him as he kept his hoodie covering his features.

When all of the police left, Sonia sat down on her sofa next to A.J. and held her hand tightly. Logan stood next to the sofa in total disbelief.

"I can sit here and scream at you both. I can lecture you and say I told you so. But what will that accomplish? You both have no idea how close A.J came to being a statistic. This is not a game. This is not a social experiment. Life here is survival. Survival of the fittest and you both are smarter than this."

"Sonia, I am so sorry. I could have just waited for A.J. like I was supposed to and..." Logan said before Sonia interrupted him.

"Coulda-woulda-shoulda. There is no acceptable excuse."

"It's not all your fault Loge, I should have called Sonia or asked you to wait for me, A.J. said. She was sipping on a cup of hot tea as she sat on the sofa, her legs folded under her.

"There is that shoulda word again. You both shudda followed my rules. There I go lecturing. Now what do we do? Do I take you both back to Ridgewood tonight? You both know that this would be the end of the road for the program, right? Sonia said.

"Let's just keep this among us. We were just careless. You were my guardian angel and probably saved my life, Sonia, but I'm okay. I'm smarter than I was an hour ago. There are bad people everywhere. Something like this could happen at home, or next year at college. I really don't want this to get out and ruin everything we've worked for. Please Sonia, I'm asking you to just..." A.J. said.

"Just make believe it never happened? What happens when you have to go to court to testify against this animal? What do I tell your parents?" Sonia said.

"I think it's time to call your friend Vic again. He will figure it out. He knows what we need to do," Logan said.

A.J. buried her head into Sonia's shoulder.

"Please, Sonia. Let's just keep it quiet. At least until after graduation. Can't we postpone things for a few months? It means so much that we don't fail," A.J. said.

"Okay. This is against my better judgment. You two have become my family, and sometimes, as a family, we need to stand together. I will call Vic, of course, and he will get things done for us. But I swear, one more knucklehead move and I will hit you both in the head like I hit that creep." Sonia wasn't kidding. The three of them hugged one another, like family.

ZIP CODE

CHAPTER 31

10468

SPRINGTIME IN THE BRONX

What remained of the winter months went by in a blink of an eye.

In May, Mosholu Parkway is in budding splendor. The maple trees along both sides of the thoroughfare are full with green, shade leaves that sway in the mild, warm wind which comes from Van Cortland Park. Here and there, the Parkway is dotted with flowering Azalea bushes and royal lavender Lilac trees.

This morning, Van Cortland Park is in its spring glory. The aroma of honeysuckle delights the senses of the joggers and soccer players who pound the luscious, green laws of the enormous grounds.

A huge, Weeping Willow and several Silver Maple trees, in full regalia on the DeWitt Clinton High School campus cast their lovely shadows and beckon the students and faculty to spend time outdoors.

Not just brick and mortar, the Bronx is beautiful in the spring.

As Logan was walking past Mr. Taveleres' office, Loida Milan was exiting. Since their night at The Point, both Loida and Logan knew their friendship could be nothing more than casual. Saying hello in the hallways and the cafeteria was as far as things went.

Loida looked stressed.

"Hey, Loida how are you?" Logan asked.

"Hi, ya. I'm glad I had this chance to say goodbye, Logan."

"Goodbye? What do you mean?"

"I have to leave school. Today is my last day at Clinton."

"Why? What's going on?" Logan asked. He could tell Loida was about to cry.

"Things are complicated with me right now. Maybe I can get my GED instead of doing my senior year next year."

"You're quitting school?"

"I have to. My baby daddy came home in February. I'm two months pregnant, Logan. I need to get a job." Loida's lips were quivering.

"Dude, you won't be the only expecting mom to be walking around the school. Can't you at least try to stick it out? Why quit?" Logan said. He felt like a guidance counselor for a second.

ZIP CODE

"I have no choice. My parents are really pissed. They want me to get my own place. I need to find a roommate and get a job and an apartment."

"What about the boyfriend? Can't he help you?"

"That's a laugh. P.P. is a gang-banger. These niggas are just good at making babies and going to jail," Loida lamented.

"He's back in jail?"

"Yeah, Rikers. Another eighteen months for parole violations. Look it, don't feel sorry for me, okay? I made the same mistake again, and I have to live with it. I must be a glutton for punishment or something. I'll be fine. Good luck, Logan," Loida said, fighting back a full cry. She left Logan standing in the hallway. He didn't know what to say to comfort her.

※

May is a busy time for high school seniors. Thoughts of exams, final grades, prom, graduation, and parties are interwoven with their last summer plans before their next big steps.

Today, A.J. and Logan were to make their final report to the Urban Planning class. Logan was in a group which included Keith Copeland and Kenny Vasquez. A.J.'s group was Junior Diaz, William Reynolds the Third, and five other students. Lamar Butler was one of the eight members of the third group.

Mr. Aaronson allotted fifteen minutes for each group's presentation. A.J. was elected the spokesperson for her group.

A.J.'s brief group summation was well received by the class. The group's written report was submitted to all class participants.

"Bridges. That is the name we gave to our presentation."

"Our inner cites are in trouble. Not only here in New York City, but all around the entire country. Detroit, Los Angeles, Philadelphia, Camden, and Ferguson, Missouri. Virtually every highly populated state has the same issues. Crumbling infrastructure, lack of jobs for the lower and middle class, drug problems, high crime related to drug addiction, corruption, and prejudice. So how do we bridge the gap between the opposing sides? How do we develop a plan for income equality and the social inequity? In our view, it all begins with changing perceptions and strong leadership.

"Whites are resenting people of color, and people of color are resenting whites. Having a black president for the first time in our nation's history has perhaps widened the gap between the political parties. Until and unless these factions meet somewhere in the middle between capitalism and socialism, and the obvious disparity which has evolved be lessened, we fear the American Democratic experiment, as we know it, is in decline and like the Roman Empire, will fall." A.J. smiled broadly at the end of her talk.

Everyone clapped.

"I congratulate the group for a job well done. You certainly didn't paint a very good picture in your summation," Mr. Aaronson said.

Keith Copeland was the chairperson for his group. His summation for their report had a different viewpoint.

ZIP CODE

"The common denominator for the problems facing Urban Developers is racism. Blacks and Hispanics have perpetuated their stereotypes by being caught up in a multi-generational failure chain. Of course there are exceptions as we see successful people of color running companies like American Express, McDonald's, Xerox, and Merck. Military and political success stories like Colin Powell and Condoleezza Rice. Supreme Court Justice Sotomayor, sports figures, and entertainers who have become icons in our culture. They are, unfortunately, a vast minority among our minorities."

"Grass roots education will be one of the key elements we have as a nation to reduce the chasm of inequity which we currently are experiencing. Education and re-education will be the building blocks we need to begin a long-term evolution for our inner cities. The time for change has already passed."

Again, applause came from the entire class.

"Another excellent report and presentation. Now for our final group, Mr. Lamar Butler," Mr. Aaronson announced.

"Thank-you, Mr. Aaronson, for the introduction and for the opportunity you have given us to make this class the most meaningful of our high school careers."

"I would be remiss if I didn't thank our fellow classmates, A.J. and Logan, for their insight and opinions of the issues we face today in the inner cities. Urban development has become, as Mr. Aaronson has previously stated, a euphemism for social inequity. Our group discussed this issue at length and came to a conclusion that may not be popular to the rest of the class.

"Many of us have felt the sting of prejudice in our lives. Unfortunately, we have done little to help ourselves achieve the greatness that we people of color are capable of.

"Just pretend for a moment, if you can, and this may be a stretch for all of us, that you are a white, middle to upper class person who has worked hard at achieving a good job, perhaps is the owner of a small business, owning property, living in a nice community.

"You hear us calling each other nigga. You hear our music denigrating acceptable social mores. Obama Care comes along and takes a chunk out of your business to pay for the medical care of the under privileged and disenfranchised. Watching the news and seeing some of our minority leaders spewing their own form of racism. We can only hope that as the ancient adage goes, this too shall pass.

"Now how would you feel? Just think about it from the other side for a moment. Personally, I, myself, and other members of our group have blamed rich, white people for our tenuous situation. We have bought into the narrative of self-loathing, of copping out on ourselves, and putting the blame elsewhere. We were very fortunate to be exposed to the other side of the coin with A.J and Logan in our lives. No more will we take the easy way out. Our group leaves this class inspired to make our world a better place in which to live. Our group agrees education and real change in our political process is the only way to have meaningful and true urban redevelopment. We promise to start right here, right now."

Lamar ended his summation by tapping his chest with his right hand, kissing his fist, and saluting to the sky. He was thinking of his mom who had recently passed.

ZIP CODE

"I must say something to everyone in the class. This group as a whole has done a fabulous job in identifying and planning a strategy for the future of our cities. You will not be unhappy with your final grades. This has been our final meeting as a class. I am leaving here with a renewed confidence in our young people. I thank you for a wonderful, eye opening experience," Mr. Aaronson said.

The class stood as one and applauded the teacher and themselves.

ZIP CODE

CHAPTER 32

07450

MAY IN RIDGEWOOD

Budding geraniums and a variety of trees abound on the Ridgewood High School campus. The sweet, fragrant aroma of peonies and hyacinth fill the afternoon air. The cracking sound of baseball bats can be heard from the Maroons' ball field. Students and faculty stroll around the grounds, basking in the sun's splendor.

Ridgewood is beautiful in the spring.

Like the students at DeWitt Clinton, thoughts of events in the month of May make hearts beat a little quicker.

"Rosa, you look fantastic. Our plan has worked wonders. I'm so happy for you," Mrs. Taylor said. Instead of taking the Range Rover, Mrs. Taylor decided on walking to the school to meet Rosa. Semaj made plans to play basketball after school. Rosa and Mrs. Taylor would walk back home together, enjoying the magnificent day.

"I owe it all to you, Mrs. Taylor. Without your guidance, I never would have dropped twenty-four pounds in four months. None of my clothes fit!" Rosa said joyfully.

"That's a good problem!" Mrs. Taylor responded. "Now we know what to get your for your graduation gift."

"You have given me too much already," Rosa replied.

"Do you have plans for prom?"

"Well, believe it or not, I've had three boys ask me. I haven't committed yet," Rosa giggled.

"No one suits your idea of a good date yet, I imagine."

Rosa covered her mouth to suppress a laugh.

"Honestly, there is one boy that I'm waiting to ask me."

"Oh, my goodness! A school crush?"

"Kinda, sorta. I hope he asks soon or I could find myself dateless, which isn't the worst thing in the world," Rosa said.

"You know, these days the girls are asking the boys anyway. Why not just ask him?"

"Nah, I think I would prefer the old-fashioned way."

"Do I know him? Sorry, I'm prying. The curiosity has gotten the best of me," Mrs. Taylor laughed.

"So what are your plans for the summer?" Mrs. Taylor asked, changing the subject.

"I'm not sure yet. I would like to go to a beach somewhere for a week or so. Maybe the Jersey shore. I've heard so much about Long Beach Island from the kids around here."

"LBI is nice. Mostly families, I thought."

"I've heard that, too. Some of the kids from Clinton are planning a trip to Montauk, Long Island. We can all rent a place together, but the prices seem very high. We can all get to Montauk by train. LBI is probably not so easy to get to from the Bronx anyway," Rosa said.

"That sounds like fun. I did that when I graduated high school. We did the Jersey shore bit. Some girls had cars, so I was able to hitch a ride. We went to Seaside Heights. I thought my parents were going to absolutely die," Mrs. Taylor laughed.

"Was it a dangerous place?" Rosa asked.

"Any place is dangerous if you go there to drink and go a little crazy. My crowd was a little nutty."

"I can't see you like that, Mrs. Taylor."

"Oh I had my wild side, Rosa. I got it all out of my system before I started college. Thankfully, I met Mr. Taylor at a school mixer my freshman year. I went to a state school. He went to Princeton. My parents were not too well off. They did the best they could. I worked my way through school. It's wasn't easy, believe me."

"Wow, somehow I thought you came from a place like you live now," Rosa blurted.

"Are you kidding? I was lucky enough to afford used textbooks. We lived very modestly. My parents still do!"

"I should have known. There is something about you that amazes me. You are so generous and kind. You are not at all snobby, if you don't mind my saying so. I guess you learned that from your roots," Rosa said.

"That has been my biggest problem when we decided on living in Ridgewood. Some of the people are just too much to take for me. Having money has never defined me. Don't get me wrong Rosa, I really enjoy the position that I'm in, but I try really hard at not being affected by having nice things."

"You've been like a mother to me, Mrs. Taylor. Even better than a mother! I'm so glad to have met you," Rosa declared.

"The feeling is mutual. You've become a second daughter to me, Rosa Colon."

Rosa and Mrs. Taylor were two blocks away from *May as Well*. A car pulled up alongside them and Semaj popped out.

"Hey guys, can I walk the rest of the way with you?" Semaj asked.

"Sure, we did all the walking and you show up for the last half-lap, typical man," Mrs. Taylor said. They all laughed.

"What a gorgeous day. I can't think of a better day ever," Semaj said.

"I agree. It's like a picture book around here," Rosa said.

ZIP CODE

"Rosa, I don't mind asking you this question in front of Mrs. Taylor. Do you have any plans for prom?"

"I have a few offers, but I haven't decided if I'm even going."

"You're going! Would you please be my prom date? I can't think of anyone I would rather go with than you."

Rosa stopped walking. She looked at Semaj and then at Mrs. Taylor and then back to Semaj.

"I thought you would never ask!" Rosa confessed.

"Great! It's a date then!" Semaj said.

As they walked up the driveway, Mrs. Taylor whispered in Rosa's ear.

"I knew it all the time."

CHAPTER 33

Thoughts of prom were the buzz at DeWitt Clinton.

The June edition of *The Clinton News* even explained the proper way to make a bow-tie.

On the same page of the school newspaper, Princeton bound senior Vidur Beharry was interviewed for being awarded a Gates Millennium Scholarship. Only one thousand students in the country can receive this prestigious and generous, full tuition scholarship. The students, faculty, administration and alumni of Clinton were all standing proud for one of their own.

Logan wasn't sure if he would attend prom. His problems with Loida made him avoid dating any of the girls at the school. He was considering asking A. J. or one of the girls from Ridgewood.

A.J. was sitting in the sun outside of the school, enjoying the beautiful spring day.

"Hi, may I join you?" Keith Copeland asked.

"Of course you may. Do you need some sunscreen?" A.J. asked. Both she and Keith chuckled at her question.

"Nah, I self-baste. That is the one major advantage of having extra melanin."

"With my fair skin I need SPF five hundred."

"So you will be going to Columbia in the fall. Are you excited?" Keith asked.

"Yes I am. And a little apprehensive at the same time, you know how it is. You will be at Hunter College, I read. I saw the listing in *The Clinton News*."

"It's not Hamilton College where Kengon and Delgato are going. And certainly not Princeton with Vidor, but I got a small scholarship. It's what I can afford, and I need to work to help my mom."

"It's a very good school, Keith. You will do great!"

"I'm a bit nervous, too. I'm the first ever in my family to attend college. I have a lot to prove to myself."

"You are very smart, dude. Your report in Urban Studies was amazing," A.J. said.

"Thanks. That class was amazing itself. We all learned a lot. I was very taken by your report, A.J."

"Why thank-you, Keith. That's very sweet to say. My group was fantastic."

"So Hunter is just a short subway ride from Columbia. Do you think we can get together? I promise not to make an ass of myself like I did at The Point."

"C'mon, stop it! You didn't make an ass of yourself at all. And yes, I would love to see you. And I can come to see you at Hunter, too," A.J. smiled.

"That would be great. I have another question to ask. I hope you don't think I'm being too forward," Keith asked.

"It depends on the question," A.J. giggled.

"Do you have plans for prom?"

"No, not yet, do you?"

"I was thinking maybe we could go together," Keith said.

He had practiced his invitation over and over in his mind, hoping she had not already had a date.

"Absolutely! It will be so fun," A.J. responded.

"Cool. I'll get the tickets."

"Dutch treat, Keith. Those tickets aren't cheap. I would feel better, anyway."

"I was hoping you would say that!" Keith confessed. They both burst into laughter.

Lucy Natal was in Logan's Urban Planning group. Lucy had admired the way he participated in the classroom and in the group. She found his shyness refreshing.

Lucy found Logan sitting alone in the cafeteria.

"Hey, may I join you?" Lucy asked.

"Sure, do you want a coke, I'm getting one for myself."

"Sure, why not," Lucy felt her stomach flip for a second.

Logan quickly returned to the table with the sodas.

"I'm just going to ask you. Would you like to go to prom together? That's unless you don't already have a date," Lucy asked.

"I don't have a date, but I though the guy was supposed to ask," Logan said.

"Is that a yes or a no?" Lucy asked.

"Yes, of course. But I insist on paying for the tickets. That would be my way of asking you, I suppose."

"Okay, but that's not necessary. We can split the cost."

"No way! I insist," Logan said.

"So it's a date?"

"Yes, it's a date. Hey, have you been to Arthur Avenue?"

"Sure, of course. But not in a long time."

"I know a great place to get the best pizza ever. Are you free tomorrow after school?"

"I work after school until seven. Does that work?"

"Sure, can we meet there?"

"Absolutely!" Lucy said. " Just to put your mind at ease Logan. I don't have any brothers and there is no gang banger boyfriend in my life," Lucy laughed.

"Geez, okay, okay. Word travels as fast at Clinton as it does in Ridgewood," Logan quipped. "But that's a relief!" They both had a good laugh.

CHAPTER 34

10458

ARTHUR AVENUE, BRONX, NEW YORK

Logan planned to meet Lucy on the corner of East 187th Street and Arthur Avenue.

The beautiful, spring day suddenly turned unseasonably chilly that evening.

Lucy was a half hour late. Logan put the collar of his Ridgewood crew jacket up around his neck as a cold, evening wind whipped around the corner. *How do homeless people deal with this cold? How can anyone survive living on the streets during the winter?* Logan thought.

Logan's cell phone beeped. He quickly removed his phone from his pocket while at the same time removed his gloves. It was a message from Lucy:

> Hi, just got off the bus at Fordham Road. Be there asap!
>
> Okay, I'm here

Logan spotted Lucy from a block away. She walked quickly, down the middle of the pavement. Instead of the way she normally dressed at school, in jeans or khaki pants, Lucy was wearing a short, leather, black jacket, a short, gray skirt with black leggings and high-heels. *Wow, she looks amazing!* Logan thought.

Logan walked up the street to meet her. Lucy smiled when she saw him. Logan had never noticed her deep dimples before. Her big, brown eyes sparkled from the reflection of the street lamps.

"I'm so sorry, Logan. I had a problem at work and then the bus was late."

"You look great. Where do you work?" Logan asked.

"Scruples. It's a women's clothing store in Riverdale. High-end, fashion stuff. It's easy to get there from school," Lucy said.

ZIP CODE

They started walking up Arthur Avenue.

"How long have you worked there?" Logan asked.

"Two years. My aunt is real good friends with the woman who owns the store. I'm real lucky to be in such a nice place. It beats working in McDonald's or babysitting, for sure. The owner lets me keep some of the latest samples, too. This outfit would cost a small fortune!"

Giovanni's was crowded. Logan and A.J. waited in the front of the store for an open table. One of the guys working the pizza oven behind a glass display counter recognized Lucy.

"Hey, how ya' doin'? Remember me?"

"Of course. Nik, right?" Lucy said.

"Yeah, how you been?"

"Pretty good, and you?"

"Better now that I see you," Nik flirted. Lucy laughed. She turned her attention back to Logan.

"He was a busboy at Patricia's on Morris Park Avenue. I worked there as a waitress for a while," Lucy explained.

"These Italian guys have all the best lines," Logan chuckled.

"Nik isn't Italian. He's Albanian. A real player!" Lucy whispered.

The waitress waived to Logan and Lucy from the back dining room. She pointed to a table and left two menus and two paper place settings with that colorful map of Italy.

"It's not fancy, but the food is good," Logan said.

"Listen to you, mister New Jersey. You really fit in to the Bronx lifestyle," Lucy laughed.

"Yeah, fuggetaboutit!" Logan said in his best-feigned, Bronx accent.

They ordered a *Margarita* Pizza and a salad.

Lucy and Logan spoke about the sudden, chilly weather to break the ice of their first date.

" So...you were the first guy I ever asked out on a date, never mind a prom," Lucy said.

"I'm really glad you did, Lucy. I wasn't even sure if I was going to go," Logan admitted.

"I can't believe you didn't already have a date. You being the most popular guy in the senior class."

"Me? You must be high!"

"No, really. You are Brad Pitt among all the girls," Lucy said. "So how did you like Clinton?" She asked to change the subject.

"I like it very much. It's a lot different than my school, but I learned a lot about myself and about people in general."

ZIP CODE

"What makes us a lot different, Logan? Really!" Lucy asked. Her tone was suddenly serious, just as Logan had seen her in Mr. Aaronson's class.

"What do you mean, 'what'? There isn't just one single thing. I can make a two page list, I guess," Logan said.

"And I can break it all down to one word...m o n e y," Lucy spelled out the word.

"Well, yeah, maybe! But that's a simplistic answer. There is so much more to our different worlds, Lucy," Logan stated.

"Okay, so start with your list," Lucy said.

The waitress appeared with the steaming hot pizza. Nik from behind the counter was right behind her with the Cokes.

"That really smells good, and I'm half-starved," Lucy said as the pizza's aroma filled the air.

"I made it special for you guys. Lucy, you were always very nice to me at Patricia's. I didn't speak much English two years ago when I came from Kosovo. You always treated me like a person and not just a lowly, bus boy. I'll never forget that," Nik said.

"Aww, that's sooo sweet Nik. Thank-you!" Lucy said.

"The pizza and the sodas are on the house. My uncle John owns this place and he's making me his partner," Nik said proudly.

"Thank you very much, Nik, that's nice of you. That's fantastic! Being a partner here, I mean."

"In a little while we will have another place, in Morris Park."

"Amazing! How rude of me. Nik, this is my friend Logan." Nik wiped his hands on his white apron and shook Logan's hand. He put his right hand to his heart as they do in his culture, as a sign of respect.

"Nice meeting you, Nik," Logan said.

"Same here. I've seen you here before, right? You're not from around here, right?" Nik asked Logan.

"New Jersey. I've been here for a few months for school. I'm going back home in a week."

"Good luck, Logan. Enjoy the pizza, you two. Say goodbye when you leave guys. If you want anything, just ask," Nik said.

"Nice guy! I think he likes you," Logan said.

"It's not like that. He's just very sweet," Lucy said.

Lucy's phone rang. The ring on her phone was an Alicia Key's song. *This Girl is on Fire.*

"Excuse me, let me take this for a second."

"Hi, Lydia. Yeah, I'm out to dinner, let me call you later, okay?" Lucy said.

Before she put the phone on silent she texted Lydia:

ZIP CODE

> This guy is gorgeous...el guappoooooo!

"Sorry, so what were we saying?" Lucy asked.

"Something about me being rich and..."

"Oh yeah. I'm trying to point out that money is the great difference between our worlds," Lucy interrupted.

"What about values? Work ethic? Stuff like that?" Logan said.

"Not all Hispanics and blacks are on welfare, Logan. I've worked since I was like thirteen. My parents never took a penny from anyone, and they taught me the same values, as you say," Lucy said. She seemed a bit annoyed.

"Look, I wasn't trying to sound..."

"Prejudice?" Lucy finished Logan's thought.

"Yeah, but I guess it came out wrong. I'm sorry."

"It's okay, I'm not insulted at all. I just wanted you to understand that we should all not be painted by the same brush," Lucy smiled at Logan. She got her point across.

"Can we agree on just one word that separated us and keep it simple?" Logan asked.

"Okay, let me think for a second. How about opportunity?"

"Cool. Look at Nik here. He has a great opportunity with this place. It's now up to him to make it work."

"Exactly! And there are a lot of us that want to emerge from our situation. All we need is a chance, and then it's up to us to work hard."

"I guess we aren't all that different after all," Logan said.

"Maybe the word luck can be used, too."

Logan and Lucy walked around to De Lillo's Pastry Shop and shared a *sfogliatelle*. They each had a *Café Macchiato*.

Logan walked Lucy to her bus stop. After a few minutes, her bus came. Lucy reached up and kissed Logan on the lips.

"I had a great time tonight. I can't wait to see you in a tuxedo," Lucy laughed.

"G'night Lucy. I had a great time, too. Hey, what color is your dress?"

ZIP CODE

"Green, why?"

"For the flowers!"

Lucy laughed. The door to the bus closed behind her. Logan watched as the bus went up Fordham Road.

Logan hailed a passing Gypsy cab.

Opportunity and luck, he thought.

ZIP CODE

CHAPTER 35

07030

PIER 13, SINATRA DRIVE NORTH, HOBOKEN, NEW JERSEY

The lavish ship, *Cornucopia Majestic* was docked at Pier 13 in Hoboken.

The guests arrived early. They began boarding at six forty-five in the evening. The ship would set sail at eight.

The girls in their elegant, beautiful gowns, all with wrist corsages, mostly white orchids, a few with red or pink roses.

The boys, all looking dashingly handsome, complete with boutonnières on the lapels of their black tuxedos. Wearing dress shoes, mostly rented patent leather, black oxfords, made the boys look a bit awkward. After all, sneakers and sandals are the choice of footwear at Ridgewood High School.

This year's prom promised to be one of the best in the school's long and storied history. Every senior attended, even the nerd group blended in well with the cool kids.

A professional photography group, hired by the prom committee, snapped away using the New York City skyline as a marvelous background for the smiling couples. Cell phones were at the ready, their owners taking group shots and selfies.

Some of the couples initially found themselves mesmerized by the ship and it's elegant appointments. They soon relaxed and loosened up to the opulent surroundings.

Rosa Colon was absolutely stunning in a sunset orange, mermaid style gown. Rhinestones adorned the gown's bodice, flickering the light into Rosa's beautiful, brown-green eyes. Her orange high-heels and a three, ruby red-flowered wrist corsage finished her striking look.

Her date, Semaj Henry, wore his tuxedo like a movie star walking on the red carpet in Hollywood. His pocket-square and cummerbund perfectly complimented the color of his date's gown. Semaj's white orchid boutonnière flattered his gleaming, white smile. His *piece de resistance* was a pair of orange sunglasses that he took from his inside jacket pocket and dramatically put over his eyes when they arrived on the ships sunny, top level.

"So how does it feel to be the prettiest lady on the ship?" Semaj asked.

"Thank-you, liar! But I can honestly say that about you," Rosa replied coyly.

"How about we just agree that we are the hottest couple here?"

"Okay, that works. I'm still trying to get used to my new figure. You have no idea how much better I feel abut myself, Semaj."

"I'm so proud of you. And thank-you again for accepting my invitation."

ZIP CODE

"Well, Denzel Washington is filming a movie, so you were my next choice," Rosa laughed. Semaj feigned a stab in the back. They both doubled over from laughter.

The evening was epic for everyone. The seniors danced all night to a great, seven musician band that did covers of *Twenty One Pilots, Taylor Swift, Childish Gambino, Time Flies, Seconds of Summer, J Lo,* and a host of other artists.

The boys ate with abandon. The girls picked at the food as birds do. Chaperones from the parent's association and a few teachers kept a keen eye on things. In spite of the diligent parents, a few flasks of contraband alcohol managed to pass their purview.

The ship sailed around New York Harbor, moving slowly for cell phone photos of The Statue, Ellis Island, and the 1,776-foot high Freedom Tower to be snapped. The glittering of lights on the skyline made a romantic scene. Some couples kissed while their friends took pictures for posterity.

Rosa took in the view of the magnificent city from the deck. Semaj stood behind her, gently holding his hands around her waist.

Rosa slowly turned, her back to the panoramic view.

"Isn't this amazing? I don't think I've ever seen anything so beautiful in my entire life," Rosa said.

Semaj, now without his prop glasses, looked deeply into Rosa's eyes.

"I haven't seen anything so beautiful, either."

Semaj kissed Rosa softly on her lips.

CHAPTER 36

The Marina del Rey sits on the Long Island Sound at the end of Tremont Avenue in the Bronx. Wedding receptions, Bar and Bat Mitzvah's, business meetings, and anniversary celebrations have made this catering hall famous for decades. Made to look like a Mediterranean villa with imported Italian Terrazzo marble, an elegant, flowing, indoor fountain, colorful hand painted friezes, and waterfront verandas, the Marina is known for their abundant food and professional servers.

Tonight, DeWitt Clinton High School's Prom shares the Marina with the three hundred-guest wedding.

"That guy who opened the car door for you has really good taste," Keith said.

"What?" A.J. asked.

"He couldn't take his eyes off you, I really can't blame him."

"Oh c'mon. Look how amazing all of our girls look. It's like a fashion show, Keith."

"I always thought this place was over the top. A little goofy, don't you think?" Keith asked.

"It's beautiful, very neoclassical. I love it!"

"I'm glad you do…then I love it, too," Keith laughed.

The parking attendant and Keith both knew a stunning young woman when they saw one.

A.J.'s emerald green, strapless, evening gown was slit in the front to her upper thigh. With plumes of small green and tan peacock feathers from A.J.'s waist to the bottom hemline, the dress was exquisite. A.J. carried herself with a sophistication that caught everyone's eye. The white orchid, wrist corsage had emerald color ribbons which matched her dress and open-toed, high heels. A simple choker of white pearls finished her look beautifully.

Keith looked like a GQ model. His tall, athletically built frame was perfect for his double-breasted, black tux. An emerald green bow-tie against his double-white shirt with faux emerald cuff links were the perfect accompaniment to A.J.'s dazzling gown.

A ten-piece house band, plus three D J rappers started as the seniors walked into the dining room.

Nobody sat at the tables until the band took a break after forty straight minutes.

"The band is fabulous! I can tell you one thing, nobody at Ridgewood can dance like our seniors at Clinton," A. J. said.

"What about Rosa and Semaj?" Keith laughed.

"Dude, you know what I mean," A.J. stated.

"Oh, you mean white people?" Keith laughed louder. A.J. faked punched his arm.

"Why, do I dance like a white chick?"

ZIP CODE

"Nah, no way. You can move."

During the band's break, the DJ tried playing softer music to get the crowd settled for a few minutes of food and soft drinks.

Sonia was one of the eight chaperones who were watching the seniors closely. She spotted A.J. and Keith on the buffet line.

"Ahh, excuse me you two. The Ford Modeling Agency party in next door," Sonia said.

"My second mom!" A.J. shrieked. Sonia hugged her and held on for a while.

"You look like a freaking, movie star A.J! You are gorgeous," Sonia said.

"Sonia, I would like for you to meet Keith Copeland, my friend and my date," A.J. said.

"You are gorgeous too; nice to meet you Keith."

"I've seen you around before. You're Rosa's mom. She is a great girl," Keith said.

"She's awight," Sonia faked a good ghetto all right.

"Have you seen Logan?" A.J. asked.

"Yes I have. Fabulous! Incredible! Hunky! And his date is off the charts. They look like they belong together, A.J. Just sayin'".

"I know! I've never seen him so gaga. I think love is in the air, Sonia," A.J. giggled.

"You guys have fun. I'm on booze control," Sonia rolled her eyes.

"Good luck with that!" Keith added. They all laughed at the futility.

Someone yelled…"Let's get this party started!"

The D J turned it up with Kanye West's, *Gold Digger*.

The crowd erupted and the tables emptied. Everyone moved toward the dance floor.

She take my money when I'm in need
Yeah, she's a trifling friend, indeed
Oh, she's a gold digger way over town
That digs on me
(She gives me money)

Now I ain't sayin' she a gold digger (when I'm in need)
But she ain't messin' with no broke niggas
(She gives me money)

Now I ain't sayin' she a gold digger (when I'm in need)
But she ain't messin' with no broke niggas

Get down, girl, go 'head, get down (I gotta leave)
Get down, girl, go 'head, get down (I gotta leave)
Get down, girl, go 'head, get down (I gotta leave)
Get down, girl, go on 'head

ZIP CODE

The crowd was going wild. The guys were lip sinking the words pretending to be Kanye, while the girls were strutting around miming to the words.

A.J. and Keith were in the center of the dance floor playing along and miming the words.

Cutie the bomb, met her at the beauty salon
With a baby Louis Vuitton under her underarm
She said I can tell you rock
I can tell by your charm
Far as girls, you got a flock
I can tell by your arm and your charm
But I'm lookin' for the one
Have you seen her?

Now I ain't sayin' you're a gold digger
I know this dude's ballin', but, yeah, that's nice
And they gone keep callin' and tryin'
But you stay right, girl
And when you get on, he leave your ass for a white girl

When Kanye said *leave your ass for a white girl,* A.J. pointed to her self, so did Keith and most of the guys and girls who were dancing around them. Including Logan and Lucy. Everyone was having a great time.

"She is really good looking, Logan. Were you and her ever….?" Lucy asked.

"Nope, never. We started in kindergarten together. We've been friends ever since," Logan replied.

"That's a relief!"

"And how about you? You said no boyfriend. True?"

"Yes, no boyfriend. Didn't have time for that," Lucy's coy reply made Logan's heart beat a bit faster.

"And now?"

"If the right guy comes along…" Lucy looked up into Logan's eye. They had a moment as they say.

Before that night A. J. and Logan had promised their parents, Mr. Spechler, and themselves that they would not be drinking at or after prom. Mr. Spechler reasoned that there was too much to lose at this stage of the program. The parents did what parents always do.

Plenty of booze made it's way into the Marina del Rey. A.J. and Logan kept to their words.

The last dance of the night was Sam Smith's slow and soulful, *Stay with Me.* There wasn't an extra inch of space on the dance floor.

> *Guess it's true, I'm not good at a one-night stand*
> *But I still need love 'cause I'm just a man*
> *These nights never seem to go to plan*
> *I don't want you to leave, will you hold my hand?*
>
> *Oh, won't you stay with me?*
> *'Cause you're all I need*
> *This ain't love it's clear to see*
> *But darlin', stay with me*

ZIP CODE

Why am I so emotional?
No, it's not a good look, gain some self-control
And deep down I know this never works
But you can lay with me so it doesn't hurt

Oh, won't you stay with me?
'Cause you're all I need
This ain't love it's clear to see
But darlin', stay with me

Oh, won't you stay with me?
'Cause you're all I need
This ain't love it's clear to see
But darlin', stay with me

Oh, won't you stay with me?
'Cause you're all I need
This ain't love it's clear to see
But darlin', stay with me

A.J. and Keith were dancing next to Logan and Lucy. A.J. looked over at Logan and smiled. It was a smile that only very old friends could understand.

ZIP CODE

CHAPTER 37

10458

BRONX, NEW YORK.

There was never a doubt that A.J. and Logan or Semaj and Rosa wouldn't graduate from their original schools. Luckily, the commencement exercises fell on different days, so the option to attend their adopted school was available if they so chose.

They all did.

A.J. and Logan were spending their last Friday in the Bronx with Sonia. They decided to have a nice dinner at Mario's Restaurant on Arthur Avenue.

A.J. sat next to Sonia; Logan sat across from the two women.

"Take my advice. After dinner, instead of having dessert here, lets just order a small pizza. Believe me, I think it's the best pizza in the entire neighborhood. Maybe the best pizza in the entire city, if you don't count Patsy's in Spanish Harlem. Then we can go around the corner to De Lillo's for a farewell coffee and pastry," Sonia said.

"Ah, De Lillo's! I've been there a dozen times since our first visit, Sonia," Logan said.

"How do you know so much about Italian food, Sonia?" A.J. asked.

"I don't. I'm a cop. We know all about donuts, pizza, coffee, and pastry. It's part of the whole life. Give me a neighborhood and I'll tell you where and what to eat," Sonia replied. "How I stay this thin is a miracle," she added.

"Speaking about thin, have you seen the selfie that Semaj and Rosa sent around? I could hardly even recognize her. She looks amazing!" A.J. stated.

"I know! She's been struggling with her weight for years. Thank God for your mom, A.J.," Sonia said.

"Speaking about thanks. If anybody deserves thanks for making this program work, it's you," Logan said to Sonia.

"Aww, that's so sweet, but what did I do?"

"Are you kidding? You let us stay at your place, you gave us the freedom that we needed to get the full experience of living in the Bronx, you introduced to us Puerto Rican food, and REAL pizza!" A.J. said.

"And you stopped me from..." Logan started to say something.

"And you saved my life, let's not forget that!" A.J. said.

"You two have become part of my family. Yes, I helped out a bit with that foolishness, but you both learned valuable lessons. I think we all did," Sonia said.

"We chipped in and bought you a present, Sonia. It's isn't much, but we thought you should treat yourself," A.J. said.

A.J. handed an envelope to Sonia. Logan and A.J. were beaming.

"Aww, c'mon, you two. That's like bribing a cop. Are you kidding? I really haven't been around that much to spend time with you guys. Between work and some personal stuff I'm going through, I really feel badly about your stay with me," Sonia said. Logan noticed tears in Sonia's eyes and looked away. He, too, felt all choked up.

"Hey, where in the narrative does it say cops can cry?" A.J. said. She reached over and hugged Sonia.

Sonia opened the envelope slowly, looking back and forth to Logan and A.J. She read the card A.J. and Logan signed with xxxs and ooos. She focused on the gift card inside the envelope.

"Oh my! I've never done something like this in my entire life! A full day of beauty at The Fountain Spa, at Riverside Square. I...I...I'm speechless. Thank-you both." Sonia now let the tears roll down her cheeks.

"And the gift includes a car to and from New Jersey," Logan said.

"Driving Miss Sonia!" A.J. said.

"This is perfect! It will be a fresh start for me. I don't mind telling you both, but I just broke off with a guy I was seeing for a while. He wasn't right for me for a lot of reasons, and I ended things last night. It's a little tough for me right now," Sonia confessed.

"Will you be able to come to our graduation at Ridgewood? My parents are coming to see Rosa and Semaj walk," A.J. asked.

"I wouldn't miss it for a gold shield!"

ZIP CODE

CHAPTER 38

10460

THE BRONX ZOO

The day after the prom of a lifetime, Rosa and Semaj met at the Bronx Zoo.

"Semaj, do you realize what we did was an experience to last our entire lives?" Rosa said.

"Yeah, that prom was somethin' else."

Rosa laughed. "No silly, I was talking about our stay in Ridgewood, with the Taylors, meeting all those great kids. Being involved with the program. I will talk about it forever."

"Dude, it was so cool. Even that stupid jewelry store thing that happened. Everyone stood behind me, you, the girls, Mrs. Taylor, great people," Semaj said.

"I wish I had a camera to film your face when you saw that the police chief's wife was black," Rosa laughed.

"Dude, I was frozen. It was an 'oh, shit!' moment for sure."

Rosa and Semaj walked slowly past the Lowland Gorilla outdoor habitat. The male gorilla was agitated and started throwing bits of apple and feces into the watching crowd. Women were screaming and running. Little kids had no idea what was happening. People were laughing and taking cover behind some trees.

"Damn, if that gorilla doesn't look just like my uncle Samuel. And Samuel is just as nasty!" Semaj joked.

"Semaj!" Rosa blurted.

"Well he does, he really does. He has that fat belly and those pissed off lookin' eyes," Semaj laughed.

"Let's get out of here before we get hit with his poop," Rosa warned.

The couple walked on. They wanted to see the tigers and seals at feeding time.

"Do you think Mrs. Taylor liked the gift we got her?" Semaj asked.

The two, soon-to-be college students had had a photo taken of the two of them at one of those places in the mall in Paramus and had the print put into a nice, silver picture frame.

"Well, she cried and held the frame to her chest. I think so, yeah. That woman is so cool. She knows we don't have much and she was very gracious," Rosa said.

"Hey, did you happen to hear what some of the Ridgewood kids have planned for the summer?" Rosa asked.

"Nah, it didn't really come up."

ZIP CODE

"Well that's what all the girls were talking about. Amazing! Steph is going to Europe on a back packing tour with her cousin. Someone is going on a cruise to St. Petersburg, Russia with her parents. Michelle is going to Rome and taking the train to Florence and Venice with a group from school. That nice couple in our Chem class are going together to the Galapagos Islands."

"There is a point you are trying to make, I feel it coming," Semaj said.

"Well, I guess I'm a bit jealous is all."

"We got a taste of the good life for a few months. Reality bites, Rosa. That's not our world."

"And I learned something about myself just recently," Rosa announced.

"And what is that, pray tell?"

"It's okay to have money, to have a life of means and achievement. I no longer want to know my place."

"What does that mean?" Semaj asked.

"I want to be successful and go to some of these places one day. If I'm going to go to med school, I'm going to work for a big hospital for a while and then open my own practice," Rosa declared.

"What about your plans to work for the emergency room and help the great unwashed?"

"I've decided to go in another direction with my life. I can still do some pro bono work for the underprivileged."

"That's a one-eighty Rosa. You sure? That's a real different life."

"Where is it written we have to stay down on the farm? I see so many Hispanics and blacks achieving great things in life and enjoying their hard work and success. So why can't I?"

"My grandfather would call that being an Uncle Tom. A house nigga," Semaj said.

"And how do you feel about what your grandpa thinks?"

"I think in his time he didn't have the opportunity to do any better. I know that I can, and with the help of God, I will!" Semaj pointed to the sky.

"I know you will. Just remember if you need a doctor…" Rosa pointed her thumbs inward.

"And you will maybe one day be the next Doctor Oz.

"That's what I learned about myself. Anything is possible. If you can think, it you can do it."

They got to the tiger and lion exhibits.

"What makes him king of the jungle? He looks sad and just keeps pacing back and forth," Rosa asked.

"Just your point, Rosa. He is caged up. No opportunity to be free, to hunt, to make baby lions."

ZIP CODE

"Amazing! You're absolutely right, Semaj. Life is so much better when you have a chance to make your own decisions. Let's get out of here. It's depressing," Rosa stated.

They took a long walk around the beautiful park, toward Southern Boulevard to catch a bus back to Fox Street.

Rosa looked out of the bus window at the poor neighborhood she has lived in all of her life.

She had a look of determination on her face.

"Life is not just this. There is a better way!" Rosa said aloud.

LOUIS ROMANO

ZIP CODE

CHAPTER 39

10467

MOSHOLU PARKWAY, BRONX, NEW YORK

"So, tell me something, Logan. Is that thing with you and Loida over? Is she out of your life?" Lucy asked.

Logan had taken his mom's car and driven into the Bronx for a picnic with Lucy. Lucy made a few things for a basket, and Logan brought along some cheese and deviled eggs him mom had made. He also brought along a cooler with soda and Evian water.

They sat on a blanket in the sun on Mosholu Parkway very near DeWitt Clinton.

"She was never really in my life. There is nothing with her and me," Logan stated.

"Did you see anyone else while you were at Clinton for almost six months?"

"Well there was a girl I met from Fordham. We went out a couple of times but I'm not into that whole drinking scene," Logan admitted.

"I'm so glad you came to see me, Logan. It's like impossible for me to visit you in New Jersey not having a car. Anyway, it's nice being with you," Lucy said.

"I'd like to keep seeing you, Lucy."

"I'm not looking for a summer fling with a rich kid, Logan. I like you and all, but I don't what to be another notch in your gun. I'm better than that."

"Who said anything about just a summer fling?" Logan asked.

"You're going far away to Princeton, and I'm going right around the corner here to Lehman College. Maybe you can meet a nice girl there. Someone more on your level," Lucy stated.

"More on my level? What is that supposed to mean?" Logan asked. He sat up from leaning on his elbow.

"C'mon, now. I don't fit into your world. You can do much better than the little Puerto Rican girl who works in the clothing store."

"Is that all you think of yourself? A girl who just works in a clothing store? You're going to college in September. Okay, it's not a big name school, but who cares? It's education and it's a start! Besides, I don't judge people by where they go to school and what they can or cannot afford. If being in the Bronx and at Clinton has taught me anything, it's taught me that we are all basically the same. Some of us are luckier than others, but as my dad always said to me…you make your own luck."

"And my being Puerto Rican?"

"Yeah, so? And I'm Irish. There was a time when my people were considered total garbage in this country. I don't care what you are, Lucy. Matter of fact I think your nationality is exciting, fun, and you are beautiful. Is that enough?"

"Well, to be very honest, Logan, I'm intimidated a little bit by you," Lucy confessed.

"Intimidated? Why?"

"Well, not about you as Logan, but about your family, and money, and all that stuff."

"Okay, so you plan to go to school, meet some guy from the neighborhood, have some babies, stay here, and just never meet your potential. Is that your goal?"

"Hell, no. I want to get into Hospital Administration. Is that good enough?" Lucy asked.

"Good enough for whom?"

"For a guy like you. Am I good enough?"

Logan stared at Lucy for a long ten seconds. He leaned over and kissed her. Lucy put her hand around Logan's neck and they kissed for a while. They both stopped to catch a breath.

"Lucy, I don't care if you work in a clothing store, run a hospital, whatever. I care for you as a person. Not a Puerto Rican person, just a person."

"We will be so far away from one another. Can that work?"

"Only if we both want it to work and we both work at it, together," Logan said.

"I would like for it to work," Lucy said.

"So would I, Lucy."

The kissing started again.

CHAPTER 40

10472

Right next to JLo's zip code..

Mr. Spechler had some difficulty setting a meeting date for the four program participants. They finally settled on a day that everyone was available.

The best place to meet was somewhere in the Bronx. Rosa and Semaj could take public transportation and Mr. Spechler would drive in from Ridgewood with A.J. and Logan. He didn't want any of the parents involved with the logistics for a variety of obvious reasons.

Mr. Spechler asked Rosa to choose a restaurant which was open for a late lunch, where they could spread out and talk. She chose *La Cocina Boricua* on Westchester Avenue near Castle Hill Avenue. It was very near to the Cross Bronx Expressway and easy to find for the New Jersey group.

The hideous traffic on the CBX made Mr. Spechler, A.J., and Logan fifteen minutes late.

Everyone hugged and kissed. They sat at a large, corner table which was graciously put aside by the owner. Colorful bull masks, and other Puerto Rican themed paintings adorned the walls of this quaint, family restaurant.

The owner brought over five menus. Rosa stopped him.

"*No me des el men, traeme todo! Estamos en famila,*" Rosa said.

"What did you say to him, Rosa?" Mr. Spechler asked.

"May I, Rosa?" A.J. asked.

"Sure, my sister."

"She said, 'don't bring me a menu, just get everything, we're here as a family'," A.J. translated.

Everyone clapped. Rosa blushed. Mr. Spechler nearly cried.

"So sorry to be late, guys. The traffic was bumper-to-bumper all the way over the bridge to here," Mr. Spechler said.

"In the Bronx, a half hour late is normal for us. You beat that by a lot," Semaj said.

"I'm so happy to finally get us all together. Rosa, this looks like a great choice," Mr. Spechler said.

"Authentic, Puerto Rican food. I hope you all like it," Rosa said.

"I'm sure we will, Rosa. We know about Puerto Rican food from your mom," A.J. giggled.

"She cooked Puerto Rican for you? Just wait until I see her!" Rosa laughed.

ZIP CODE

"So, here we are. I must say, all of your weekly reports were very well written. They were like a slice of life from both schools. All of your writing quite brilliantly captured your experiences. I would like to go around the room and ask you all what you learned from the program. Then I'm going to make my observations and make an announcement that may blow you all away. Who wants to begin?"

"I'll start!" Semaj said. "I had some preconceived notions about the whole program. I was very apprehensive about living in Ridgewood. To me, rich...or shall I now say, affluent people always made me feel a bit uneasy. I never thought I was good enough. I though these white people always looked down on me, thinking I was a thug or a hooded, hip-hop gangster. I didn't find that to be the case at the school. Everyone treated me as Semaj, not the black kid...just Semaj. Only one time did I feel the sting of bigotry. You all know about what happened to us at the jewelry store. I was really pissed off. I held my temper, and thought this is exactly what I had expected. Mrs. Taylor stood right by me, as did Rosa and our friends. It wasn't until that night when the police chief, Mr. Grabowski, came over to us in a restaurant and apologized to me, that my bitterness left me. When he introduced his wife, a black lady, I felt horrible for having those negative, racial feelings."

Semaj continued. "I can tell you the schoolwork is way harder at Ridgewood, and the academic demands are like, bam, in your face. I only hope that Clinton will one day be at that level."

"Me next?" A.J. asked. Mr. Spechler nodded.

"Where do I start? Socially it was a rough beginning for me. Frankly, I was petrified. No, really, I was. The subways, the amount of people on the streets, not seeing many people like myself, you know, white people, was very offsetting. Thank God for your mom, Rosa. She gave us some very good advice for the streets. I had no idea that I shouldn't engage in a conversation or respond with creeps on the subway or those who drove by in cars and trucks. That was my first, big hurtle. Then in the classroom, I had to refrain from saying that we had already learned the material like a year or two ago. I agree with Semaj. Clinton will have to step up their academics over time. I know they are trying and it's a process, but that was one big thing for me. I must say, I walked away from this experience a new person. I now have a true understanding that people are people and should not be judged by their economic status."

"Rosa? How about you?" Mr. Spechler asked.

Some of the food came and everyone asked what each dish was. Rosa did the explanations.

"Sure, perfect timing. I get to speak and the food comes out," Rosa said. She and everyone had a good laugh.

"Well, that's a pretty good segue. I always had low self-esteem. Sure, I'm a good student, that was easy. I didn't go out much. I had few friends. Books became my friends, my escape, from how I was feeling about myself. I really caught up to the work once I figured out the pace that I needed to apply. It wasn't until a few girls in the senior class asked me to hang out that I felt part of the school. I would have been content staying home and just reading and studying. That would have been an awful mistake."

Rosa went on, "Then an off-hand remark about my weight sent me into a depression. It really did," Rosa confessed. She paused to gain her composure. A.J. reached over and touched her arm.

"It really hurt. But I needed it. It wasn't that I was Spanish or poor, or from the hood, it was that I was fat that bothered me. Semaj, you were wonderful through my whole process of evaluating myself. I love you for that. I reached out for help and found my guardian angel. A.J., your mother is an absolute, magnificent, loving...I just can't say enough without making us both cry. I guess I couldn't get that kind of relationship with my own mom. She never really knew how I felt about myself. Or maybe, I don't know, maybe she was okay with me being a little roly-poly. Perhaps she thought that would be a defense mechanism for me. Well anyway, I did what I had to do, with help, and I will never look back. I also changed my mind about staying in the hood. I discovered it's okay to have money and still be your own self. I learned that from my New Jersey mother as well."

"So, I see you saved the best for last!" Logan announced. Everyone clapped.

At that moment, more food came. It looked delicious, but the group wanted to hear from Logan before they dug in.

"I loved the experience. I thought that, yes, the schoolwork was way below what I was used to. But so was the pressure on the students. One of the worst things about my time at Ridgewood was seeing so many people so stressed out because the pressure they had from their parents. I'm not so very lucky; the work does not comes easy to me. Just think of the kid who is struggling to make a B average, but with parents who think he or she needs to go to an Ivy. I know a bunch of kids on drugs. No, not illegal drugs. Prescription drugs. They need to be medicated to cope with the pressure. From the second or third grade, some of the parents are putting kids on the big name college track. What happens to the student who just isn't all that academically gifted? Think about what happens in their minds. I've lived it, and it's no picnic. I met a lot of good people at DeWitt Clinton. They have their own set of life issues to deal with. I'm just not certain yet which ones are better than the others."

Logan paused, then continued.

"I also learned a great life lesson. To always surround yourself with good people. People you can trust who care about you for the right reasons. Rosa, you mom needs a medal for how she helped me out of a sticky mess. You should be very proud to be her daughter. I love that woman. And she takes no shit!" Logan said.

Everyone laughed again.

Rosa stood up an announced the *comidas*. "Ok, family! These are *empanadas*, this here is *mofongo* Rican style, rice and beans of course, *pernil*, that's roast pork, *Chicharron de pollo*, fried chicken, *Chuletas*, grilled pork chops..."

CHAPTER 41

The meeting at *La Cocina Boricua* went on for a while. The owner brought out a selection of his homemade desserts. Rosa flat out said no, but pointed out which desserts were her favorite. As it turned out, they all were.

Tembleque, a coconut pudding, *Arroz con Dulce*, "The Puerto Rican answer to rice pudding, but better," Rosa proclaimed. *Dulce de Papaya*, and a tasty *Bizcocho de Ron,* a rum cake.

"Okay, Mr. Spechler, it's your turn. You said you had an announcement. We are dying to hear it!" A.J. said.

"First of all, because of you four, brave, and caring students, this experiment...our program, exceeded my wildest expectations. I think everyone who touched any of our lives, in both schools and both communities came away learning something that will have a positive effect on the rest of their lives. Your parents, neighbors, classmates, store owners, police, virtually anyone you guys came in contact with on a daily basis."

"Just think for a moment how this kind of thing can go viral. Imagine if the walls of prejudice weren't so high anymore, and opportunity for everyone became more exposed to better education, better employment opportunities, less racial conflict.

"I'm Jewish. My family wouldn't hear of me marrying a non-Jewish woman. Many people could not marry someone outside their faith or ethnic background or race in this country for a very long time. That kind of thinking kept people down, so they could not emerge in society. You guys have begun to bridge the gap between the economic disadvantaged, the disenfranchised, and the upper end of the economic spectrum. I say begun because there is a long and bumpy road ahead for our society. In a way, you are pioneers, and I applaud you for the magnificent job you all did."

Another round of applause erupted.

"Okay, now the announcement you have been waiting for with baited breath," Mr. Spechler said in a dramatic, almost Shakespearian voice.

"A while back, I made a presentation to a large group of teachers and educators in Chicago. My discussion has been heralded in those circles throughout the United States. I am preparing my final lecture on the program, and I will present it next month to Congress," Mr. Spechler paused dramatically and took a sip of water.

"Ahh, excuse me. Congress, like THE Congress in Washington?" A.J. asked.

"Yes, you heard it right. The legislators in Washington who can do something to help students throughout this country."

Spechler continued.

"Even more important than Congress, the media has gotten ahold of our experiment. I have been invited to be interviewed by several prime-time, news programs and guess who is interested in having us all on her program? Oprah Winfrey herself. I want you guys to consider coming on the media tour with me if you can. And then to Congress."

"Holy crap!" Logan said.

"No trip to Europe for me. Italy and Spain will always be there," A.J. added.

"I just can't!" Rosa said. "I just can't believe this, I mean," Rosa said.

"Talk about fifteen minutes of fame!" Semaj blurted.

"I will let you all know the schedule as things progress but here is an amazing turn of events we just agreed to do. We, meaning the Ridgewood Board of Education and the Board of Ed of New York City through Mr. Taveleres.

"Film crews from the major networks and two, investigative news magazine programs will be at both of your commencement exercises," Mr. Spechler said. "Oh, and The New York Times is sending a reporter."

"Sooo cool!" Semaj declared.

"Needless to say, this is all good stuff for your resumés. We made the big-time guys!" Mr. Spechler pronounced.

"Oh, I thought you had something important to tell us," Logan said.

The group went hysterical with laughter. High fives were given all around.

"Oh, sorry, just one more thing. I'm about to sign a book deal about the program. Just sayin'".

"A book…a real book?" A.J. said.

"Yes, a real book." Mr. Spechler replied.

"What's the title going to be?" Rosa asked.

Mr. Spechler paused for a moment.

"I'm not sure yet…any ideas?"

"How about ZIP CODE!?" Rosa said.

"It's all about that, isn't it?" Mr. Spechler said.

To the Reader:

Author **Louis Romano** endeavors to have ZIP CODE bring about healthy discussion on what each of us can do to make the world a better place. It is his hope you will find a way to have open discussions about the questions put forth below, while understanding some of them are only for inner reflection. Please use the two formats *discuss* and *reflect* simply as a guide, and only share that of which you are comfortable.

Thank-you

Chapter 1

Reflect In chapter 1 we are introduced to the affluent neighborhood of Ridgewood, New Jersey. Have you ever felt pressured to "keep up with the Joneses?"

Have you ever heard someone you look up to and respect mumble something disrespectful? Do you think you were affected by that? *Discuss* Have you ever thought about those less fortunate than yourself? What does your community offer in which you could volunteer or donate time/money?

Optional activity: Grateful journal

Why was there silence when Mr. Spechler told the affluent group of students and parents there would be two students coming from the Bronx to live in their neighborhood? Would you go? Would you host? Would you automatically trust or would they have to earn your trust? Would you want them to trust you?

Do you know of anyone who started with nothing and became famous and/or wealthy?

If you live on the west coast, what have you heard about those on the east coast, and vice versa? Do you actually know these things to be true? Would you hold a prejudice about a group of people based on what others have told you about them~ just based on their geography?

What is a scholarship?

What is a cracker neighborhood?

Have you ever considered what it would be like to not graduate? Do you believe your environment has something to do with your success or failure in the future? How so? What would it feel like to be around people who couldn't or didn't care about graduating? Would you find it difficult to remain strong? On page 6 of paragraph 2, the author gives the first jolt of what it feels like to be from a poor neighborhood. Entering into a neighborhood which could be hostile towards them. Is that something you've ever thought about?

First glimpse into walking in their shoes how would you want them to feel? They will leave forever having experienced your neighborhood. What would you want them to remember? Would all the people in your neighborhood feel as you do?

The meeting before the meeting~ Even in higher class situations, there is a priviged hierarchy. Would your parents let you go?

If yes, what would be their motivation?

Chapter 2

Discuss how the parents handle the situation about their children growing up in the world.

Chapter 3

Have you ever been to a camp or away from your parents or guardians for an extended period of time? What preparations were made? Why?

On page 17, Mr. Taylor tells Mrs. Taylor A.J. is no push-over. What does that mean?

Discuss street smarts vs intelligent smart. If you were the parents of a boy would you feel differently than if you were the parents of a girl?

Have you ever wondered about the safety of someone?

Pg.19 Logan tells his parents their world has passed. What does he mean by that? Do you think your parents ever had decisions to make with which that their parents (your grandparents) disagreed?

What does Mr. Darby mean when he says they ARE better than most people?

Chapter 4

Discuss In chapter 4 we see the underprivileged kids enter their new home for the semester. How did they feel there? Did Mrs. Taylor make them feel welcome and deserving? If yes, how? If no, what could she have done?

What does Mrs. Taylor say to Rosa that is positive? to Smaj?

Chapter 5

Discuss Sonia is eating with AJ and Logan on the night before their first day in the Bronx school. Both A.J. and Logan have expressed excitement and being scared. Why? Have you ever been excited and nervous to try something new? How did you overcome your fear? Did you have anyone supporting you or was it you, alone? *Discuss* the alone-ness of the book's cover.

Chapter 6

Discuss Why does the Bronx have a bad reputation?

What does Sonia tell them they must do to be safe? Do you think you should be extra cautious just because it is a "bad" neighborhood?

Logan is reluctant to say the word "white" referring to A.J. and himself while walking in the Bronx. What phrase does he use that shows he is starting to realize what it's like to be prejuduced against?

Sonia gives A.J. and Logan her thoughts on what she hopes will be their take away from living in the Bronx. What is it?

How can people from different countries break barriers with open discussion like the characters are having? Do you know of any outreach/integrative programs in your own community?

Chapter 7

Reflect What have you done to reach out to those less fortunate than yourself? Mentor/tutor/donate food/take in homeless/paid for someone's meal. What are some things we can put into practice?

Chapter 8

Discuss It becomnes clear to A.J. when she sees roaches on a daily basis, urine in the subway, and has to use public transportation that life for the disadvantaged isn't always in their control. Have you ever had a pen pal from a different part of the country or from another country? Share

Chapter 9

Google and make a list of programs in your area which work to conquer gang violence, anti-bullying, etc. Pick one and get more information for possible future involvement

Discuss How do young people handle growing fears of stepping out into the new world?

Chapter 10

Discuss Rosa and Semaj are greeted warmly at their new school. They are both clearly touched and appreciative of the efforts put forth on their behalf by the Ridgewood moms. Who else will benefit by what these moms have done?

Chapter 11

Reflect A.J. showed prejudice toward someone with a tatoo. Have you ever made judgment about someone based on their appearance?

Discuss Does the news media and/or social media's actions reinforce that? How might people be influenced by those situations?

If you were to visit another country where they spoke a different language, you would educate yourself about that. If someone tells you a certain city or neighborhood was unsafe, what would you say to them?

Chapter 12

Discuss Different cultures bring us different foods. Why? Have you ever gone to an ethnic group's heritage parade or festival? What did you learn?

Discuss Selfies- Are the two worlds different in that regard? What happened?

Chapter 13

Discuss Mrs. Taylor seems more involved as a parent to her boarders than Sonia. Why do you suppose that is?

Rosa admits she is feeling inferior. Semaj quotes Eleanor Roosevelt: "No one can make you feel inferior without your consent." Have you ever been the subject of put downs? If so, how did you overcome it? Did you have help and/or support from others?

Besides Semaj, ONE person changes Rosa's outlook. Melissa calls and invites her to go somewhere. Have you ever felt out of place and somebody invited you in? Have you ever thanked that person for the profound input they had on your life? What can you do/say to make someone's day better?

Chapter 14

Discuss Logan, speaking with "black" slang mockingly and A.J. chastises him. They both realize they have been influenced by what they were exposed to possibly by their parents. Have you ever been around someone who is mocking another due to their weight, looks, intelligence, etc? Have you ever been an innocent bystander while someone else has been harrassing another? If yes, what did you do?

Chapter 15

Discuss Rosa has some ups and downs. Do you think she says she wants to stay in the "hood" as an excuse in case she tries and fails?

Rosa and Semaj discuss "white people problems" of anxiousness, pressure to succeed, grass is always greener. Should people stay in their own class? What does Semaj offer for advice?

Chapter 16

Discuss A.J. is "amazed" Loida has her head on straight. Why?

Music seems to be a common denominator between the cultures.

What other things do you think teens/young adults have in common?

Compare and contrast wage earnings, employment, education, divorce statistics.

Chapter 17

Discuss Semaj and Nicole~ Notice Semaj impresses her with his knowledge of history.

There may be unintended consequences when we speak to others~ for good or for bad. Discuss the results from someone being fat-shamed vs compliments for someone trying to lose weight. Which would you prefer?

What positive impact can you leave for someone? How?

Chapter 18

Discuss Why does Rosa feel comfortable confiding her problem with Mrs. Taylor?

ZIP CODE

Chapter 19
Discuss Sonia helps Logan with his relationship, Vic helps Sonia with her relationsship. Is it wise to surround yourself with good mentors you can trust?

Chapter 20
Discuss Rosa and Michelle. Michelle apologizes for being insensitive to Rosa. Rosa, instead of being angry, accepted the apology and they both made a postive out of a negative. How might this have turned out differently?

Chapter 21
Discuss Ephraim is protecting his sister. In the "hood" protection may involve life or death consequences. He has difficulty trusting. Logan lied to Sonia and violated that trust. How does lying damage a relationship?

Chapter 22
Discuss The choice of language between Kathy Darby and Mr. Spechler about Logan's incident with Ephraim was "approached" vs "accosted". How might these two versions of the same story influence someone hearing the story? How is the media responsible for reporting the news?

Mr. Darby uses foul language and Mrs. Taylor admonishes him. Mr. Spechler uses his skills to diffuse the situation by reminding them of the bigger picture and they move forward. How else could this have turned out?

Chapter 23
Discuss Rosa thinks Semaj is being patronizing about her weight when he starts singing to her. When you compliment someone is it genuine? Is false praise worth anything?

Chapter 24
Discuss Urban Planning. How has urban planning/development changed over the years? Was what was being done not working or did the needs change?

Can you invite your local urban planning person to come and speak to your group?

Chapter 25
Discuss Semaj is the victim of gossip. Have you ever been the victim of gossip? How did you feel? Have you ever been influenced by gossip

others told you about someone? Did you like or not like that person based on what someone else told you about them? What can be done to 1) eliminate gossip? 2) not be influenced by what you hear?

Chapter 26

Discuss how Mr. Spechler's experiement has far less to do with acadamia than it does social mores.

When the parents see each other's houses what record is still playing in Sonia and Delores' minds about their ability to get out of the Bronx? Why did they make up jokes about naming their own houses?

Mr. Taylor said good bye to his Jaguar because he parked it in the Bronx. What expectations do they have? High? low? What expectations do you have for yourself?

Chapter 27

Discuss Back at his own home, Logan is greeted by his friends with racial comments about Semaj. He has taken a more serious, mature tone and admonishes his friends. Have you been brave enough to speak up even against a group of people who may have taken on the 'mob mentality'? Do you think one person can bring about change to make the world a better place? Would a person's conscience be bothered if he/she kept silent?

Chapter 28

Discuss the racial issue when Nicole makes a cruel remark to Semaj about "his people" but he hears Rosa's record playing over and over in his head.

Discuss the jewelry store incident Might it have turned out differently if Michelle hadn't spoken up? What if that had happened the first week of school when they hardly knew him? Why did the store owner respect Mrs. Taylor? Was it because she was white, wealthy, or both? Do you think it would have had the same outcome if Mrs. Taylor wasn't rich? Do you think she was respected just because she was white?

Chapter 29

Discuss racial profiling. The student body and school administrators rallied around Semaj. From that incident, Lilly realizes her own prejudice and is crying. Why would she be crying?

The police chief's wife is black. Why do you think the author included that in the story? How would that affect Semaj's beliefs when his new friends texted him and told him they didn't think the same way the store owner did.

Chapter 30

Discuss A.J. and Logan reach out to form study groups. They want to cover each others' backs. When A.J. gets accosted, Sonia has her back. Social media today allows us to see a lot of fighting. If you witnessed a fight, would you stand there and film it? Do you think uploading it to social media helps, or does it cause more apathy as viewers see others standing around filming instead of intervening?

Chapter 31

Discuss Loida is pregnant. Does it appear that cycle is being repeated, or does she have the same chance to escape poverty as anybody else?

If you were in charge of the city, what programs would you implement so as to have possibly prevented the pregancy in the first place? Should birth control be available?

Bridges presentation- Keith Copeland cites black people running huge corporations, and he goes on to thank A.J. and Logan. The author cites Supreme Court Justice Sotomayer. Who do you thank?

Chapter 32

Discuss the bonding between Mrs. Taylor and Rosa~ Is it easier to talk to people besides your parents? How do you know who you can trust? Does reading this book, knowing parents have their reasons and possibly even some experience with life you may not know about, make you want to listen to them more?

When Rosa and Semaj decided to go to prom together, were you disappointed thinking they didn't get dates outside of their "social class"? Should it matter?

Chapter 33

Discuss There is an old-fashioned sense when Logan says he is paying for prom. Social mores appear to be changing for some. How do we know which ones to hang on to and which ones we should discard? Make a list of old-fashioned vs new thinking mores in a social setting and see which ones you like or don't like. Do you think it will be more important that another person holds those same values you do, no matter where they're from?

Chapter 34

Discuss Lucy is treated in kind because she had treated that same person kindly in the past. She explains to Logan she thinks *opportunity* and hard work are keys to success. Do you agree? *Discuss* It's not what you know, it's who you know

Chapter 35
Discuss Amongst the wealthiest students in the country, Rosa and Semaj enter their prom with confidence declaring they are the hottest couple to attend. From where did they get their confidence?

Chapter 36
Discuss At the dance, A.J. is dancing with her date and Logan is dancing with his when they both make eye contact with each other as "only very old friends could understand." What do you think they were thinking?

Chapter 37
Discuss the thank-you and gift of appreciation given to Mrs. Taylor by Rosa and Semaj. Does the price of the gift matter to Mrs. Taylor? How do you know?

Chapter 38
Discuss Rosa and Semaj reflecting on their experience.
What will they do in their future? Is that changing from what they first thought?

How can a person make themselves more open to opportunities which may come along?

How were they treated and how did they treat others?

Share your thoughts on the analogy of caged animals, and the Bronx and breaking free.

Chapter 39
Discuss Logan and Lucy. Does Logan think he's dating beneath himself? When Lucy says she's intimidated by his family and money, does Logan worry about what his parents might think or is he making his own decisions? How would you deal with parents who strongly objected to your date or marrying someone?

Chapter 40
Discuss trust. Surround yourself with people you can trust and who care about you *for the right reasons*. Identify some of those reasons.

Chapter 41
Imagine if the walls of prejudice were down. What do you think the characters would do next? Write to the author by commenting on his Facebook page and let him know what you think! What will YOU do?

ZIP CODE

CPSIA information can be obtained
at www.ICGtesting.com
Printed in the USA
FFHW021610130219
50499289-55775FF